HIS WIN

BY

ANGEL RAYNE

His Win
Copyright © Angel Rayne 2022
All Rights Reserved

This is a work of fiction. Names, characters, places, events, organizations, and incidents are either products of the author's imagination or are used fictitiously. Any resemblance to actual persons, living or dead, or actual events, is purely coincidental.

No part of this book may be reproduced, or stored in a retrieval system, or transmitted in any form or by any means, electronic, mechanical, photocopying, recording, or otherwise without the express written permission of the publisher, except for the use of brief quotations in a book review.

Thank you for respecting the hard work of this author.

Published by Everblood Publishing, LLC
https://everbloodpublishing.com

ISBN-13: 978-1-945499-63-0

Cover Design by Maria Christine Pagtalunan @ https://artscandarebookcoverdesign.com/

Copy Editor: Mackenzie @ NiceGirlNaughtyEdits.com

ALSO BY ANGEL RAYNE

Mafia Romance Reading Order

Luca and Veda

His Game

His Stakes

His Win

Enzo and Sera

His Promise

His Rejection

His Proposal

Dark Romance Stand Alone

Tyler and Ailee

Be With Me

SYNOPSIS

**The cards are on the table, and I'm
betting *everything* on her…**

My *vita* betrayed me. Sold me out to my worst enemy.

If she were anyone else, she'd be dead. But killing
her would destroy me, so I gave her a chance to run. She
took it.

I never should have let her go.

Now, everything I've worked for is within reach. I'll soon
have not only my revenge, but also my rightful place in
the business.

And none of it means *anything* without Veda.

Winning her back won't be easy. She'll resist me and the
dark desire that draws us together at every turn.

But I won't stop until she's back in my life—and my bed
—forever.

Because in this broken, violent, dirty fairy tale, it's
the *monster* who'll get the happily ever after...

CHAPTER 1
VEDA

*R*UN.

And I did. Like the fucking coward I was.

However, I couldn't escape the look of betrayal I saw on Luca's face, or the fear and loss that darkened his blue eyes right before I ran out of his office. That look would haunt me for the rest of my days.

And there was pain. So much fucking pain. Both his and my own.

But you know what? I was pissed off, too. He wouldn't even listen to me. He'd allowed me to explain, but he didn't *listen* to me. He didn't care that I was scared. That I'd only done it to try to protect him. And I half wondered if the only reason I got out of there alive was because he didn't have a gun handy and he couldn't quite bring himself to kill me with his bare hands.

My heart raced as I had Enzo drop me off at the bus station and went inside, watching in a state of disbelief as the SUV pulled away. Right before I'd gotten out of the car, he'd shoved a piece of paper at me with his number on it, along with a large wad of money, telling me to use it for a ticket so there'd be no paper trail and Luca wouldn't be able to find me.

"Be smart. Don't do anything that'll give him a chance to track you, because he will. And honestly, Veda. I don't know what the fuck he'll do when he finds you." He paused. "Take care of yourself, and hang onto that," he told me with a nod at the paper. "Memorize that number and then burn that piece of paper. If you ever feel your life is in danger, call me immediately. Otherwise, I don't want to hear from you. Oh, and hey"—he grabbed my arm before I could get out of the vehicle—"just because we're letting you go doesn't mean we've forgotten about you. But you need to get far away from here. And you need to forget about *us. Comprendere?*"

I nodded. I understood exactly what he was saying.

But I had no intention of going anywhere until I made sure my parents were okay. Until I told them about Nicole. And Sammy. I needed to check on my best friend. And I needed to talk to her. Warn her. Tell her what had happened, despite Enzo's warning. I trusted Sammy with my life. She wouldn't tell my secrets. She was the most trustworthy person I knew. Besides, as soon as she saw me, she'd know something was wrong, and if I knew Sammy—and I did—I could guarantee she'll harass me about it until I tell her exactly what's going on...

Oh, god. I couldn't breathe. My heart was shattered. And I didn't think it would ever be whole again.

An hour later, scared, tear-stained, and desperately needing a shoulder to cry on, I showed up on my best friend's doorstep with the one suitcase I'd thrown together before Enzo had rushed me out of the house. She'd started classes at the University of Texas last fall, and had an apartment that she shared with two other roommates.

"I'm sorry I haven't called you," I told her as soon as I finished hugging the ever-loving crap out of her. "My phone broke a while back and I haven't had a chance to get another one." The lies slipped so easily from my mouth these days.

She took one look at me, flipped her long, purple braids over her shoulder—so pretty against her dark skin—and pulled me inside the apartment. "I figured your sister was running you ragged. You look like hell. But not your usual *I work too much and need to get my own life* kind of hell. You look like the kind of hell only a hot guy...or girl"—she glanced up at me with curiosity. I shook my head with a rueful smile, and she sighed and continued—"can cause. Lucky for you, I just stocked up on ice cream."

I laughed. I couldn't help it. It was such a cliché thing to say. And she was dead fucking serious when she'd said it. "I've missed you," I told her.

Sammy smiled. "I've missed you, too. Now get your skinny white ass into this kitchen and tell me what the hell happened since I last saw you."

"I'm not skinny." The words were automatic. We'd been having this same argument since we'd met.

"Girl, you are nowhere near as thick as me. Although I know you wish you were..." She rubbed her hands down her hips and thighs suggestively. The smile fell from her face when I just looked at her and didn't roll my eyes and give her my usual comeback. I felt lost. Like this entire conversation was all a dream of a past life. One I didn't know anymore. One I didn't belong in.

"Shit, V. What the hell is going on with you?"

An ugly laugh burst from me as fresh tears welled in my eyes. "You won't believe me when I tell you."

She watched me struggle with my composure for a few seconds, then said, "Look. How about we get you settled in my room. You can wash your face or get a shower or whatever you need to do to pull yourself together while I order some food. And then we'll talk."

"I don't want to put you out. I just needed a place to stay until I could see my parents and I didn't know where else to go. I can't stay there with them. Mom is...well...you know..." I shrugged. "She fucking hates me."

"Pfft. Girl, please. Who the hell are you even talking to right now?" Grabbing the handle of my luggage, she started hauling it to the back of the apartment, talking the whole way. "I'm the one who found this place, so I got the biggest bedroom. And the biggest bed. *And* my own bathroom. There's plenty of room."

"Where are your roommates?" I asked as I followed her down the hall. The apartment was larger than I'd first thought, but still cozy. An open kitchen with a breakfast nook and living area took up the front of the space, all white and beige and bright and airy. The furniture was also done in light colors. Nothing fancy. Just a cream-colored sectional couch that wrapped around a long coffee table with a big plant on one end and a window on the other, a television, and some neutral artwork on the walls. Down the hall were two bedrooms across the hall from each other, a closet, and a bathroom. Sammy's room was at the end. The entire place was carpeted, except the kitchen and bathrooms. "This place is nice," I told her through my tears as I followed her into her room.

"It's better than a dorm room." She hefted my suitcase onto the bed. "The roomies are at class or work or somewhere other than here. We don't really keep tabs on each other, which is why I like them. That, and they're never late on rent. Although I do have to get on Ian sometimes when it's his turn to take out the trash."

"Ian?"

"Yeah. He's got the first room on the right. Maddie has the other one."

"I take it Maddie isn't your current fuck, since she has her own room and all."

Sammy gave me a smirk. "Maybe we just like to sleep in our own beds. Jealous?"

"Always," I told her.

"Ah, if only you liked girls, V. I'd ruin you for anyone else."

I gave my best friend a sad look. She was probably right. She was totally hot. With this confident vibe that made gay girls flock to her and straight girls question their sexuality. And the girls she hooked up with never wanted to leave. "I wish I did. I really do. Because I've had enough of fucking men right now."

Without a word, Sammy closed the space between us and gave me another hug. I wrapped my arms around her, inhaling her smell that I loved so much. Some lotion she'd used ever since I could remember. "I love you, V," she told me. "But, girl, you stink like you've been walking the streets all day. Get your fine ass in the shower and then we'll stuff ourselves with greasy food and you can tell me all about this boy who broke your heart."

Boy. Luca was far from a boy. But I didn't bother to correct her. She'd find out soon enough. Pulling away, I grabbed some clean clothes out of my suitcase while she went to order food.

Two hours later, we were sitting on the couch. The coffee table was littered with empty takeout containers, two shot glasses, tissues, and a half empty bottle of pineapple vodka, and Sammy was looking at me like she'd never met me before. I'd told her everything, only leaving out things that might pull her into my mess. Like names or locations.

I finger-combed my hair away from my eyes. "What?" I asked her.

"V, don't take this the wrong way, but maybe you should do what he told you to do. Maybe you should run."

I shrugged one shoulder. "I did. I came here. He doesn't know anything about you."

She barked out a laugh. "If you believe that, you're almost as stupid as your sister." Immediately after she said it, she slapped a hand over her mouth. "Oh, shit. Fuck. I'm sorry. I forgot for a second."

I pulled her hand away from her mouth and held it in mine. "It's okay. She was a bitch. But she was my sister and now she's dead. It takes a minute to get used to."

Squeezing my hand, she let it go and leaned back against the couch cushions. She was quiet for a long time as she stared at the blank screen on the television. "V, what if he finds you here? Or worse, his crazy-ass brother. What was his name?" She stared off into the distance, like she was trying to remember.

"I didn't say," I whispered. "And stop trying to trick me." I didn't even tell her the worst parts about him yet. I didn't show her the carving on my chest or go into too much detail about my time spent with him. That was a conversation for another time. "He won't find me. I made the guy who took me out of there think I was getting on a bus. And I don't have a cell phone, so there's no way to track me. I'll go out tomorrow, though, and pick up one of those pay-as-you-go phones."

Sammy got up and started pacing back and forth on the other side of the coffee table. "Veda, I don't think you get it. You're in some really deep shit here. You need to get out of the city."

"I understand better than you think," I told her. "But I can't go anywhere until I can get my parents somewhere safe, and I was hoping you could help me."

She frowned at me. "How the hell am I supposed to help you? I'm a broke college student."

"I don't need your money. Just a place to crash until I can make sure they're safe and get out of town. And maybe your credit card to buy plane tickets." The one upside of not having a life of my own while I worked for Nicole was that I'd managed to build up a good savings account. Now that I'd cried myself out, at least temporarily, my mind was spinning. I couldn't transfer money into

Sammy's account or her PayPal because they'd be able to track it. I'd have to just pull out the cash and give it to her. But I couldn't do that until the last minute, so if the transaction was tracked here to Austin, we'd all be well on our way somewhere else. I shook my head. No, that wouldn't work either. Our names would have to be on the tickets. They'd still track us...

I sat up and put my head in my hands. "Fuck. No. That won't work either. They check everything with IDs. There's no way I could sneak them out of here on a plane and my mother wouldn't step one foot onto a bus. It'll have to be a car." I looked up and found she'd stopped pacing and was standing over by the window, peering down at the street in front of the building. "If I give you cash, can you buy a car for me?"

She turned around. "I can do that."

"Thanks," I mumbled, my mind still going over all of the ways I could possibly escape the city. "I can't put anything in my parents' name, or the people looking for me might think I'm with them. I'm not worried about him." I didn't have to say which "him" I was talking about. "He wouldn't hurt my parents..."

"Are you sure about that?"

I looked up to find her eyes on me, one perfectly waxed eyebrow lifted in disbelief. "I am," I told her. "It's not him, but his brother I'm worried about. The only one he would be after is me. But his brother?" I didn't even want to think about it. "Who knows what the hell he'd do if he found out I was gone. The guy is literally crazy, Sammy."

She started pacing again. I watched her wear a path on the living room carpet, stopping only to grab the bottle of vodka and take a swig.

What the hell was I even doing here? I could be putting her life in danger. "Look, if you don't want me to stay, I get it. It's okay. It was stupid of me to come here. It's just that you're my person, Sammy. And I just need a little time to figure things out. And call my parents." I looked down at my lap and played with the hem of my shorts. "God, they don't even know about Nicole."

Sammy stopped pacing and turned to face me, the bottle hanging loosely from her hand. Her expression was sympathetic, but worried. "What are you gonna tell them?"

I lifted my head. "The truth. Kind of. I'm going to tell them Nicole got mixed up with some bad people and was killed in Mexico. And that I've been in hiding because they were worried whoever went after her will come after me, being that I look so much like her." I chewed on my thumbnail. "I'm just not going to tell them who 'they' are."

"I don't like this, V. You need to go to the cops. Hell, the FBI! Let them put you in protective custody for real."

But I shook my head. "No. I can't do that. I *won't* do that. They'll just want to use me for info on him." I tried to make her understand. "I know what he is, Sammy. But

I'm not turning him in. I can't. I'll cut off my hair. Change my name. Make myself unrecognizable. It'll be okay."

"Are you sure about that?"

I didn't answer.

"Veda..."

"No." I stood up and started picking up our trash. "It'll be fine. It will." I stopped on my way to the kitchen and turned around. "I won't stay long. I promise. And I'm sorry for bringing you into this. Honestly, I didn't even think about it when I came here, Sam. I just needed you. Needed to get my head on straight before I went to see my parents. But if it's too much, I can go to a hotel. It's not an issue. Really."

Sammy scrubbed her face with her hands, then dropped them to her sides and gave me "the stare." The one she gave me when she thought whatever I was about to do was the worst idea she'd ever heard, but she was gonna support me anyway because she was my ride or die and that's what we did. "You can stay as long as you want. I love you. You know that. I can't just throw you out there to the wolves."

No. She would never do that. Not like he did. I gave her a small smile. "Thanks. And I love you, too."

"But I'm putting you on the chore list," she called out as she plopped back down onto the couch. "And you're chipping in for groceries."

"I'll even pay you for the water and electricity I use," I told her as I came back for the last of our takeout containers. "As soon as I can pull out my money."

But Sammy waved away the suggestion. "I'm just fucking with you. I'll loan you a little to get a phone. You can call your parents and whatever else you need to do. Then we'll worry about everything else."

Walking over to her, I bent over and kissed her on the cheek. "I'm lucky to have you."

"Yeah, yeah. I know."

I smiled as she picked up the remote to find us something to watch. Even though tomorrow, neither one of us would remember what it was.

CHAPTER 2

LUCA

"*I* think she's innocent." Tristan held the punching bag as I hit it. "Well, not completely innocent. But I've decided I believe what she told you, that she was only snooping around your office because she felt she had no other choice."

I couldn't even feel my hands anymore, my knuckles busted open and bloody even with the tape wrapped around them, but I wouldn't stop. Couldn't stop. Not yet. Because as soon as I did, my recent actions—and the repercussions of those actions—would come crashing down on me again. I'd chased Veda out of the safety of my home. And now I didn't know where she was, or if she was safe. Or if she was even alive. And it was driving me out of my fucking mind.

"I don't wanna fucking talk about it," I growled.

He was silent for a full minute this time before he started in again. "But I think we should. I think we need to." He stared at me from behind the bag, brown eyes revealing nothing of what he was feeling. But Tristan felt plenty. I knew this, as did Enzo, being the only two people who had ever seen the man behind the mask, if only on seldom occasions.

However, right now, I was too overwhelmed with my own pain to worry about his. With a roar of rage that sounded more like something that would come from a cornered animal, I let everything inside of me explode, punching and kicking the bag so hard Tristan had to dig his feet into the floor to avoid being thrown into the wall behind him. And when I couldn't hit it anymore, I hugged the bag and drove my knee into it, imagining it was my brother's face. And at times, my father's. A few times, it was even Tristan's.

"Are you finished?" he asked me when I finally staggered back away from the bag, my chest heaving and my muscles trembling with fatigue. Sweat dripped into my eyes, and I swiped at them with the back of my forearms. How I wished my mind would become as blessedly numb as my knuckles. Not even the copious amounts of alcohol I was about to drink as soon as I got to my office helped with that. Not completely.

"Luca, we need to figure out where she is."

"No. We don't."

"We need to find her."

I spun around so fast I nearly fell over. "We need to *find* her?"

He released the bag. "Yes," he answered.

For a long moment, I stared at him like he was out of his fucking mind, then I limped over to the small fridge. Bracing one hand on the top so I wouldn't fall over, I bent down and swiped a water from the shelf inside the door, then slammed it closed and fell into the chair beside it. I studied my friend with eyes that burned from too many sleepless nights. "What the fuck are you trying to do to me, Tristan?" He knew as well as I did what would happen if I found Veda. What I would have to do. I'd have no choice. Not if I wanted to maintain any level of respect with the family.

As far as I knew, right now, the only ones who were aware Veda was no longer under my protection were me, Enzo, and Tristan. Hopefully, it would stay that way long enough for her to get somewhere far away. "And why the fuck do you suddenly care?" It was usually Enzo who rode my ass about stuff. Not this guy. Tristan never said shit about shit. Just followed my orders and was content to be around us.

He held both hands up, stopping my tirade before it started. "I know. I know. I'm the one who wouldn't give her a chance to explain herself before I called you. The only one who believed you did the right thing by sending her away. But I've had men watching your father's house, and Mario's place. She hasn't gone to either of them."

With the clues Veda had given us and a lucky break or two, Enzo had managed to figure out where my brother had held her, though he was no longer in residence. It was an apartment complex in a less populated area northeast of the city. He'd rented out every apartment on the top three floors, which was why no one had heard her scream, if her version of what happened was true. But I was still plagued with doubt. I couldn't get the thought out of my head that maybe she'd been in on it the entire time. That she was the bait my brother needed to fuck me so good he'd never have to worry about me again. Maybe I was meant to find her that day. Exactly where she was outside of her sister's apartment.

A wave of shame and disgust washed over me. Maybe she'd been with him from the start. "She wouldn't need to. There are phones. And from the look of things when I arrived, you got there before she was able to find anything to tell them. But that doesn't mean it was the first time she snooped around my office. It doesn't mean she isn't a rat for Mario."

He got down on the mat and placed the bottom of one foot against the inside of his opposite thigh. Then he reached over his straight leg to stretch his hamstring. "Or maybe she did it because she believed she was saving your life."

I chugged down some water, letting his words soak in. I wanted to believe that. He had no fucking idea how much I wanted to believe that. But goddamn it. This *was* my life on the line. The lives of my people. I scrubbed my face with my hand and shoved my wet hair back off my forehead, ignoring the pain in my knuckles. As much as it killed me to admit it, my fucking father was right. I couldn't trust my own instincts when it came to Veda. That woman fucked with my head just by smiling at me. And I would tear down this entire fucking house piece by piece with my bare hands just to hear her smart mouth and watch the storms gather in her gray eyes again.

To feel the way she touched me, part innocence, part fire.

"Luca, we don't even know where she is. Anything could've happened to her after she got on that bus. She had no time to plan, to get money."

"Enzo gave her money."

"And how long will that last her?"

Enough. I couldn't think like this. I had to be smart. "Jesus Christ, Tristan. Would you listen to yourself? I don't *want* to know where she is. I *can't* know where she is," I told him. "She fucking *betrayed* me." I slapped my palm against the center of my sweaty chest, the pain in my voice evident, even to my own ears. The pain I refused to acknowledge except when I was alone with a fifty-dollar bottle of crap whiskey because Lisa said she refused to waste money on anything better when I was just going to gulp it down like water and use it to self-medicate. "I can't bring her back here, Tristan. You know the rules. There's no mercy for a rat. And there are no exceptions. It's bad enough I let her leave this house walking on her own two feet." I paused, my upper lip lifting in a sneer. "Except the rules, apparently, don't exist for my fucking brother. At least, as far as my father is concerned. But you know as well as I do his body parts should be scattered across the desert for the vultures right now. My father is soft where Mario is concerned. And he's also a hypocrite. I can't show Veda the same mercy or he'll belittle me for the same exact fucking thing, and I'll never have a chance to fix everything he broke within this family or keep him from having my psychotic brother take over as boss."

Tristan swapped his position and started stretching out the other leg. He was silent again as he tried to think of a way to convince me. And I knew him well enough to know he wouldn't stop until he had.

I took a drink of my water as I waited, my eyes drawn to the scars on his arms that disappeared beneath the short sleeves of his white T-shirt. Scars he let no one see other than me or Enzo. He never talked about them, and after one attempt that had ended badly and almost cost us both our best friend, we stopped asking about them, figuring he would open up to us eventually.

And yet, I'd known him for most of our lives, and he never had. Not once.

Without taking his eyes from the floor, he said, "As soon as Luigi finds out she's not here, he'll go after her. And we both know that he'll also tell Mario. If your father and brother get to her before we do, she *will* be dead, Luca." He met my eyes.

"She's a rat," I repeated, though there was no heat behind my words this time. He was right. If my father found her, she was dead. Or worse. He would probably let his men do whatever the hell they wanted with her before they chopped her up into little pieces and sent me pictures. It would be his way of twisting the knife in my back.

My lungs clenched around the rock of ice sitting heavy in the center of my chest as the image of her face came to me, her skin ghostly white, her lips pale blue, the blank stare of death in her eyes.

Luigi held all of the cards right now because I'd thrown down my hand and walked away. But I didn't give a shit anymore. Let him win. I was done with him and his fucked up games. Growing up with him as my father? It made me almost as twisted inside as he was. I was well aware of this fact. But I didn't have to become him. I was stronger than my father. Stronger than my brother.

"Luca, you can't mean to just leave her out there defenseless. I know you're angry at her. I *know*," he repeated when my eyes flashed up to his. "But will you be able to live with yourself if something happens to her?"

I didn't answer him. "I need a shower." Rising on unsteady legs, I left him in the gym and slowly made my way up to my bedroom. On the way, I silently prayed to God that I'd be able to get through this.

But as soon as I walked into the room we'd shared, Veda's scent assaulted me. It was there no matter how many times I had Lisa clean it. It permeated the walls, the rug, the bed, everything in here. It greeted me every morning when I opened my eyes and every night when I stumbled up here to fall onto the mattress in a drunken stupor, hoping this time I'd consumed enough alcohol to sleep.

I saw her everywhere. In the shower, as I was now, all I had to do was close my eyes and she was there in the smell of the shampoo, her skin soft and slick under my palms. My closet was full of her clothes I wouldn't let anyone move. At the dinner table, I felt her foot touching mine, heard her voice and her laughter and her moans of pleasure from the night I tied her to her chair. I saw her smile in the candlelight. The flames dancing in her eyes, mesmerizing me until I couldn't look away.

In my bed, I smelled the scent of her skin and remembered the taste of her cunt. The way her eyes flashed right before she lost herself to the pleasure I wouldn't allow her to deny herself.

She was nothing but a ghost now. And she haunted me.

I prayed she would never stop.

CHAPTER 3
VEDA

"Hi, Dad." My voice broke when I said his name, and I pulled my new phone away from my ear until I could get a grip on myself. Sammy had picked it up for me this morning before she went to class. We decided I should stay away from the stores to minimize the chance of someone seeing me coming and going from her place. At least until I saw my parents and filled them in on everything they needed to know and could decide what I was going to do.

"Hey, honey! Long time no hear from you." My father laughed at his greeting. The same way he always did every time I called him since I'd moved out of his house when I was eighteen. It didn't matter if it'd been a day or a month since he'd last spoken to me. "What the hell's going on with your sister? We haven't been able to get a hold of her for months, and your mother wanted to talk to her about the upcoming award ceremony." He lowered his voice. "You know she's always bugging me to buy her some fancy gown, even though I keep telling her Nicole won't want to take her mother as her date." Back at normal volume, he said, "I know you two are busy, but the least you can do is give your dad a call once in a while and let me know you're still alive."

So my parents didn't know about Nicole's engagement either. I wasn't really surprised. The only thing they ever watched was HBO or Netflix, and neither one of them read the news. "Yeah, I'm sorry about that, Dad. There's been a lot that's happened these last few weeks." I tucked my free hand under my arm to stop its shaking and paced Sammy's bedroom. "Are you guys free sometime today?" I needed to tell them about Nicole. And no matter what kind of danger I was in, it just wasn't something I could do over the phone. They deserved to hear everything in person. Well, not everything. I planned to skim over a lot of it where I was concerned. But Sammy had caught a ride to campus and left me her old Honda so I could go to their house. I planned to borrow something of Sammy's to wear, including something with a hood I could pull up to hide my hair.

"Of course, honey. You wanna come over for dinner? I don't know what your mother's making, but I'm sure it's something you'll like."

That wasn't true. My mother went out of her way to make the things Nicole liked. She'd never once asked me in all the time I could remember what I liked to eat.

Lucky for her, I wasn't very picky. "Um, actually, I was wondering if you two would be home in about an hour."

There was a moment's silence. "What's going on, Veda? Where are you?"

"I'm at Sammy's. And I just haven't seen you guys in a while, and..." I took a breath. "There're some things I need to tell you."

"I'll have to check with your mom, honey. You know how she is. But I'll be here, of course. Anytime you need me."

"Dad, please. I need to see you both. It's very important. And besides, my lesbian friend won't be there, so Mom doesn't have to worry about it."

"Veda..." He drew out my name. "You know that's not..." He stopped and sighed. "Ah, hell. What's the point? I mean, I love your mom. But she's not perfect. I guess by now there's no sense in denying how she feels about your choice of friends."

Wasn't that the truth. My mother had never liked any of my friends. Even in kindergarten, I tended to find the kids who were just a little too weird for everyone else for whatever reason—their haircut, their finances, their sexual orientation... "It's okay, Dad. I do know how she is." I wandered over to the window and peeked through the blinds. The street below was empty. Just the usual cars parked up the street. "So, are you gonna be home?"

"Uh, yeah. We should be." I heard him shuffling around in a drawer for something. "I'll let your mom know you're coming over and make sure she stays here."

"Okay. I'll see you soon."

"Sounds good." There was a pause. "Veda? Just tell me. Is everything okay with you and your sister?"

"I'll talk to you when I get there, Dad," I told him after a pause. Then I ended the call before he could ask me any more questions.

I closed my eyes and took a shallow breath, then another, until I no longer felt like I was going to pass out. Alone in Sammy's apartment, there was nothing to distract me from the fact that my sister was dead. Nothing to take my mind from the circumstances that led to me being here.

Circumstances. That word wasn't enough to describe the force that was Luca. And it didn't even begin to describe what my life had been like these last few weeks.

Unconsciously, my hand went to my chest, and I rubbed the new scar that was there. He'd torn me away from my life, shook my world like I was inside of a snow globe, and then let everything settle as it may before sending me away to pick up the pieces by myself. And what was I supposed to do? Just go back to my life like nothing had ever happened? Like these past weeks didn't exist? Like *he* didn't exist? The life I had before I'd met him was gone. And I wasn't the same girl I'd been back then.

I had no idea who I was now.

An hour later I was circling the block of my parents' house, checking for any strange vehicles parked on their road. I had no idea if anyone was actually looking for me here since I supposedly got on a bus, or if anyone would be watching their house. But I didn't want to take any chances. When I didn't see anything unusual, I circled back to their house and parked a few houses down. I waited a few minutes before I got out of the car, tracking any activity going on around me, and then I jogged up the small alley beside the house I was parked in front of and cut across the next yard so I could sneak in through the back. It was the same way my sister and I used to sneak out when we were younger.

My dad was the one who answered the back door. His handsome face lit up when he smiled, and he pulled me right into a bear hug. "There's my girl," he said, dropping a quick kiss on the top of my head before he pulled away. "Changed your hair, huh? I don't know if I like it. It's too much like your sister's now, and that was the only way I could tell you and Nicole apart from a distance."

It wasn't true. I normally outweighed my sister by at least 15 pounds, although it might be a little less than that at the moment, and we had completely different taste in clothes. Always had. "Hi, dad." I couldn't bring myself to smile back. The weight of the news I had to tell them weighed so heavily on me I wanted to blurt it out and get out from under that burden, but another part of me wanted never to have to tell him. "Where's Mom?"

His gray eyes, so like my own, traveled over my face. He frowned. "She's upstairs. I'll go get her."

The house smelled just as I remembered, like my father's cigars and my mother's flowery perfume. I went over to the fridge and grabbed a bottled water while he went to fetch Mom. I wished it was vodka, but there was no alcohol in my parents' house, not since my mother had discovered clean eating and yoga ten years ago. It really put a damper on our teenage experimentation. At sixteen, we had to pay one of Nicole's friend's older brother to buy us beer from the corner store. And the only reason I was included was because I had the majority of the money.

"Veda. What are you doing here?"

I plastered a smile on my face and turned to face my mom. Blonde like my sister and I, she had strands of gray running through her long hair now. "Hi, Mom." There were no hugs. No kisses. She just stood there on the other side of the counter in her expensive active wear and waited to see why I had interrupted her in the middle of her day. "I'm sorry to just drop by like this."

"Nonsense." My dad sounded genuinely offended. "You're our daughter. This is your home. You don't need a reason to come here."

My mother stayed quiet.

"Anyway," I went on. "I have something I need to tell you." Tears filled my eyes, and I had to take a few seconds before I could talk. "Um, it's about Nicole."

"What have you done?" my mother whispered.

"Nancy!" my father admonished her. "Let Veda talk."

I stared at her, and I wished I could say that I was surprised by her remark, but I wasn't. Other than being born with a heart defect, I had no idea what I'd ever done to deserve her hatred, but now wasn't the time to get into it. I looked at my father. "Nicole is gone," I managed to get out before my voice caught. "She...she was killed. In Mexico."

I watched the color drain from his face as he stared at me in disbelief. "What...in Mexico...I don't understand..."

My mother was unusually quiet, and when I glanced over at her, she was staring at me like I'd just grown a second head. "If this is true," she said while my father struggled to understand what I'd just told him, "why are *you* telling us this and not the authorities?"

"Mom, it is true. I'm so sorry." Unable to hang onto the little composure I'd had, I burst into tears before I'd even finished what I was saying.

"I don't understand," my father repeated.

I just shook my head. "She's gone, Daddy. I'm so sorry."

"No. Not my little girl. No." His face crumbled, and he reached for my mother, who still stared at me like I'd lost my ever-loving mind.

I kept talking, hoping to get through to her. "She was in Puerto Vallarta. At a spa," I improvised. I couldn't tell them she was at a rehab facility. I didn't even know if that was true or somewhere she'd been forced to go so the press couldn't get to her. "She was...shot...in an alley. They shot her. She must've screamed for help, or..." I threw up my hands. "I don't know why."

My mother hadn't moved an inch, and her expression hadn't changed. "How do you know this?"

I couldn't lie to my parents. "Because Nicole had gotten involved with some bad people. She was...engaged."

"Engaged!" my father exclaimed.

"Yes," I told him. "I didn't know. I'd never even met the guy before she sent me an invitation to be in the wedding."

"You were with your sister constantly." My mother waved away my explanation. "How could you not have met him?"

"Because he's a criminal, Mom. And I think she knew I'd try to talk her out of it."

"A criminal?" my dad repeated. Tears ran down his cheeks as he tried to comprehend what I was saying.

"I've been in hiding ever since, because I look so much like her. They're afraid the ones who killed her will come after me. Thinking I'm her," I explained. I didn't bother to clarify that "they" were criminals also. And that I had fallen in love with one of them myself.

"Oh my god." My father wandered over to the table and clumsily sat in a chair. A few seconds later, heartbreaking sobs echoed through the kitchen. For a moment, I couldn't move. I'd never heard my father cry like that before. Walking over to him, I bent down and wrapped my arms around his shoulders. We cried together for our loss, my father hanging onto me like a lifeline as my mother stared at us like bugs under a microscope.

When our grief was exhausted, I got up and grabbed a box of tissues from the counter, then took them to my dad. While he cleaned up his face, I turned my attention to my mother, wiping at my own tears. "Mom, I'm so sorry..."

"How long have you known about this?" she asked me, completely dry-eyed.

"What?"

"How long have you known?" she repeated.

I tried to think. "A few weeks now, I guess." I tried to pinpoint the time and couldn't. "I was in hiding—"

"And you couldn't even pick up the goddamn phone and let me know my daughter had died?"

"Nancy. That's enough." My father tried to reprimand her, but there was no anger in his tone. Only grief.

I stared at my mother. She was angry at me. "No. I couldn't. I wasn't allowed. Are you angry because I didn't tell you right away, or because it was Nicole who died and not me?"

"Veda, you know that's not true," my father said.

I ignored him. This was between my mother and me. For my entire life, she'd made me feel like I wasn't good enough. And why? Because I'd been born with a heart defect? I'd never understood why she'd nurtured Nicole and discarded me. And I don't know if I ever would.

"I'll believe this when I hear it from someone official," she decided. "Perhaps your sister just got tired of you and ran off somewhere with her new husband."

My mouth fell open as she turned on her heel and walked out of the room. A moment later, I heard her stomping back up the steps.

"Veda." My father's comforting touch landed on my shoulder. "She's just in shock, that's all." I heard the tears in his voice.

"She forced me to work for her," I said to the empty place where my mother had stood. "She never let me have my own life. I was Nicole's fucking errand girl. I did everything for her." My voice rose as anger mixed with my grief, until I was screaming at the ceiling. "If anyone would want to run away, Mother, it would be me!"

"Honey, calm down." My dad wrapped his arms around me. "She's in shock, Veda. That's all. She's in shock. As am I."

I turned my face into his chest, my tears wetting the front of his shirt. "Why does she hate me, Daddy?"

For once, he didn't try to defend her. "I have no idea, honey. But it's not your fault. You've never done anything wrong."

And with that, I exhaled, all of my anger leaving me as quickly as it had come on. I just didn't have the energy for this right now.

"Come sit down with me."

He took my hand, and we went into the living room, where I answered his questions as best as I could without telling him anything he didn't want to know. I told him they would release her death certificate as soon as they caught the guys who killed her, and he took me at my word. "I have to be careful not to lead them to you, Dad. So I can't be here a lot."

"Can you call at least?" he asked. And his gray eyes were so desperate and sad that I found myself nodding.

"Whenever I can."

I stayed with him all afternoon as we cried and remembered and smiled through our grief. It was healing to sit there with him. Something I didn't realize I'd needed until just that moment. He didn't ask about her body, and I was grateful, because there was no body to bury. But he did want to plan a memorial service. I agreed to stay in town until then and help as much as I could.

My mother never came back down.

When I left, promising him I would call soon, I snuck back out the same way I'd come in. The sun was just starting to set, and I was anxious to get back to Sammy's apartment. I felt too exposed out here in the open.

I was halfway back to the apartment when I noticed the same car had been following me since I'd left my parents' neighborhood. I kept driving as my mind raced. It was probably no one. But what if it wasn't. My heart thundered in my chest as I took a sudden left, heading toward the highway and away from Sammy's apartment.

The car behind me followed, nearly hitting an oncoming car in the process.

I was being tailed. "Shit. SHIT."

CHAPTER 4
VEDA

$\mathcal{I}$ kept my speed steady as I tried to think.

I could go to the police, but what would I say? "I'm being followed. I think. And it could be the guy who'd kept me prisoner in his beautiful lake house these last couple of months or his crazy brother who carved his initial into my chest. Most likely the latter. No, I'm not on drugs."

Well, there was one way to find out. One hand on the wheel, I took the piece of paper Enzo had given me out of my pocket and then felt around on the passenger seat until I found my new phone. Carefully, I entered his number.

"Yes."

I almost started crying again when I heard his voice. "Enzo? It's Veda. Is Luca having me followed?" As weird as this situation was, I trusted him to be straight up with me. Enzo and Lisa were the closest things I'd had to friends while I was at Luca's, and neither one of them had ever lied to me that I knew of.

He didn't even hesitate. "No. Where are you?"

My heart, already racing, picked up speed. "I'm in Austin. I never got on the bus. I'm on I-35 on the north side of the city, heading south."

I heard him cursing softly. "Goddammit, Veda."

"I know."

"No. You fucking don't know. What the hell were you thinking?"

"I'm sorry!" I cried. I glanced up at the rearview mirror. The car was getting closer. "I couldn't leave without telling my parents about my sister. I went to their house today to tell them. I was so careful. I swear it!"

I heard his heavy sigh. "What is the car doing? Are they trying to hurt you?"

"No. I don't think so. They're staying about two car lengths behind." I glanced back at the road and then back to the rearview mirror. "What do I do?" I cried.

"Just keep your speed steady and tell me why you think they're after you and that this isn't just a coincidence? I don't want to alert anyone to the fact that you're still here if I don't need to. You get me?"

"Yeah," I told him. Then I cleared my throat and checked the cars behind me again. "It's a black car with tinted windows. Even the front. I first noticed it right when I left my parents' neighborhood, but I wasn't sure. So I made a last minute hard left to get on the highway in the opposite direction and they did the same. They almost caused a three-car pileup to stay on my tail."

He cursed again. "Okay. Just keep driving. Keep your speed the same. I'm going to tell you how to get to Luca's club."

"I don't want to see him," I rushed to say. "Enzo, I can't see him. He'll kill me."

"Veda, you have to come to the club. I won't be able to get to you in time any other way, so you're going to have to trust me. It's the safest way. Now I'm going to tell you how to get here. Are you ready? Can you remember?"

I glanced up at the rearview mirror again. They were still there. "Yes." I listened to his directions as he repeated them twice. I repeated them back to him, then I hung up the phone and put it back on the passenger seat.

The car followed me until I pulled into the parking lot of the strip club, found a spot, and parked. I watched in my mirrors as it slowed down to cruising speed. My hands shook on the wheel as it stopped on the street to my right. I was reaching for my phone to call Enzo again when it suddenly sped away.

Someone knocked hard on my window, and I screamed, slapping my hand over my mouth when I saw that it was Enzo. He gestured for me to get out of the car, and then scanned the area around us with one hand on his gun as he waited for me.

I grabbed my keys and my phone and got out of the car. As soon as I was beside him, Enzo tucked me under his arm, and we ran to the door. I kept checking over my shoulder, half expecting someone to jump out and grab me. But we made it there with no incidents.

As soon as we were inside, a small cry escaped me, and I threw myself into his arms. He smelled like the forest at night. But I barely noticed. I couldn't stop shaking.

"Shhh...it's okay," he told me. "You're okay. Hopefully, the security cameras got the plate number. We'll find out who it was." He took me by the arms and held me away from him. "Veda, you see that hall in the back of the club?"

I wiped at my eyes and glanced in the direction he pointed. "Yes."

"The office is down that hall. Go there and wait for me."

The bouncer, a big guy with scary as fuck tattoos on his face and neck, leaned up to say something in Enzo's ear, and he nodded.

I stayed where I was, torn between wanting to run to the back of the club or back out the door. Luca was here. I could feel it. "I can't see Luca. You know what he'll do to me, Enzo."

Enzo straightened and looked down at me with an unreadable expression. "You're safe here. I promise you. Now go. I don't want you out here in the open in case they decide to come back."

Well, that got my ass in gear.

Circling the tables directly in front of the rectangular stage, I dodged a few drunken hands from the patrons as I made my way to the back of the club and down the hall. Girls shook their money makers on the stage and others wandered through the crowd, but I was too distracted to notice much.

The office door was closed when I got there. Hesitating for just a moment, I put my hand on the knob and turned it.

The doorknob was ripped from my hand as the door was pulled open from inside the office, and I found myself face to face with ice-cold blue eyes. Seconds ticked by as we stared at each other, the sudden well of pain in my chest rising to form a knot in my throat. Tears stung my eyes as I took in everything about him, from his messed up hair and bloodshot eyes, to the way his black jacket hung loose and wrinkled off his shoulders. Unconsciously, I swayed toward him, my blood racing through my veins in anticipation even as I knew I had to get the hell out of there.

With a sob, I turned to run, but I didn't make it. His hand wrapped around my arm, and I was dragged into the room.

The door shut behind me with a loud click, muting the sounds of the club. And I wondered if I'd ever come out of that room again.

CHAPTER 5
LUCA

I stared into Veda's terrified expression as her fear washed over me in waves. Even after everything she'd done, I didn't enjoy the sensation. "Hello, *amore*."

Other emotions flitted across her expressive face. Denial. Anguish. Anger. That last one is the one that stuck. It only took her a few seconds to find her spirit. She tried to pull her arm from my grip. "Let me go, Luca."

"I told you to run," I growled at her.

"I did."

"Not far enough."

She pried at my fingers with her other hand, and I released her, only to shove her back up against the door with my forearm across her chest, my knife open and the blade pressed flat against her throat. Reaching around her with my other hand, I turned the lock.

When she felt the cold steel of the blade against her delicate skin, she stilled. Her gray eyes grew wide and pleading. "Luca, please."

I searched her face for evidence she was guilty of the crimes I'd accused her of. But all I saw were her clear gray eyes and sweet mouth, begging for my kiss. My upper lip lifted in a snarl. "What the fuck are you doing here? Do you *want* to die? Is that it?"

"No," she told me quietly. "Of course not."

"Then why the fuck are you still in my city? Why are you *here*, at my club?"

Her eyes focused on my left shoulder. She didn't hesitate with her answer. "I couldn't leave without telling my parents about Nicole. And I needed to do it in person. Not over the phone."

"And did you tell them?"

"Yes," she whispered as tears pooled in her eyes. "Today." I stared, fascinated, as they became as luminescent as the Mediterranean Sea right before a storm.

"And yet, you're still here." I pressed the sharp edge of my knife against her soft skin. Not enough to pierce the tender flesh, but just hard enough to get her attention. "Running right into my arms, no less."

Her eyes shot to mine, and I saw a flash of white teeth as she snarled, "I wasn't running to you. Now let me go."

Ah, there she was. I smiled.

My eyes fell to her throat, then lower to the baby pink short-sleeved shirt she wore with frayed jean shorts. I could see her white bra through the thin fabric, the tops of her breasts overflowing the cups.

A sudden, sharp ache in the center of my gut made it hard to breathe. "Veda." Her name was nothing more than a whisper, but it contained so many things I felt inside that I couldn't name or explain, even if I wanted to. And over it all was an overarching need to have her writhing underneath me. To feel the softness of her breasts and belly against my chest and hips. To watch her as she came, when she was real and raw and completely her, and there were no secrets between us. To hear my name torn from her in such a way, I knew it was both a curse and a prayer.

I felt her drawing away from me, and I wanted to scream with frustration and need. "Luca...don't." But there was no real venom behind her words this time.

"Don't what?" I asked, my eyes never leaving her luscious body. I turned the point of the knife until it slid beneath the neckline of her shirt.

"Don't do this." Her voice was barely audible over the heavy bass of the music out in the club, even as close as we were. "I can't do this with you."

With a quick jerk, I sliced her shirt from her neck to her heart. Closing the blade, I put it back into my pocket, grabbed the edges of her shirt with both hands, and tore it completely open, revealing the "M" carved into her chest that still made me fucking insane every time I saw it. The urge to possess her—to prove who she belonged to—rushed through me, making my cock swell and my stomach twist with need.

My hands found her breasts as she tugged at my wrists. But it would take much more than that to make me stop touching her now. I thought I'd never see her again. And now she was here, her body cold and shaking against mine, her skin damp from the humidity outside, and the warm scent of her filling my nose. Fuck, I could practically taste the salt of her skin on my tongue.

I squeezed the giving flesh that more than filled my palms. Perfect. They were fucking perfect. *She* was fucking perfect. There wasn't anything about her I didn't hunger for. Didn't crave with every fucking cell. Her body, her mind, her sassy mouth. She both soothed my soul and fired my blood. She distracted me. Tantalized me. Made me burn until I could think of nothing but her.

I needed to feel more of her bare skin in my palms. Could think of nothing but the hard bud of her nipple in my mouth. A moan escaped me as I remembered the taste of her pussy on my tongue.

"Luca! Stop!"

I heard her deny me. Felt her hands clawing at mine as she tried to get out from between me and the door. But the words were far away, muted behind the rush of blood roaring in my ears and the frantic beat of my heart. My god, I'd missed her. Missed *this*. I needed to be inside of her. Needed the physical connection that was the only way I could show her what she did to me. How fucking crazy she made me. And how lost I was without her.

Yanking down the tops of her bra, I exposed her breasts to my hungry eyes. And then my mouth was on her, sucking one nipple into my mouth and then the other, rolling it between my teeth, Veda's cries in my ears even as she tried to fight me off. But it wasn't enough. Wasn't nearly enough. I eased the pressure of my hips, and my fingers went to the fastening of her shorts. I pushed them down over her ass and hips until they were on the floor around her ankles. Her virgin white panties joined them as she struggled against me. She could fight me all she wanted to, but I would bet my life they were soaking wet.

I wrapped my hands around her hips to hold her against the door and dropped to my knees, ignoring her ineffectual fists as they landed on my head and shoulders. My focus was on the sweet flesh between her legs. I could smell her arousal. Taste it on the back of my tongue. And my mouth watered like I hadn't eaten in a month. Using my thumbs, I separated the plump lips. She was wet and swollen, as I knew she would be, despite how she tried to deny her need for me.

With the first touch of my tongue, her body jerked, her ass hitting the door before her hips rolled forward to press herself against my mouth. I moaned aloud as her fingers tangled in my hair and pulled, the pain only adding to the lust raging through my blood. I was so fucking hard, but I needed her to come in my mouth more than I needed to be inside of her right now.

Fucking hell, she tasted even better than I remembered, and I wished more than anything she would spread her legs so I could reach more of her. As if she heard my unspoken thought, she lifted one foot out of her panties and shorts and rested her leg over my shoulder, opening herself up to me.

"Good girl," I told her, my mouth still on her pussy. I licked her from back to front until the proof of her desire coated my tongue. Then I found the hard bud of her clit again, satisfaction filling me as I soaked in her cries and felt her knee give out until the only thing holding her up was me. My groin tightened as she exploded, coming hard in my mouth. I drank her in, and thirsted for more.

But she hadn't said my name.

Rising to my feet, I lifted her from the floor and wrapped her legs around my waist while she was still coming down from her orgasm. I kissed her, nipping at her lips until she opened for me and could taste herself on my tongue as I reached one hand beneath her ass to undo my slacks. I groaned aloud against her mouth when my cock sprang free, lining up the swollen head with her pussy. I was so worked up for her I was ninety percent positive I would come the moment I got inside of her. But I couldn't stop. Couldn't give myself a moment to get my shit together. I needed her too much. I'd missed her too much.

Holding myself at the base, I lowered her onto my cock, inch by agonizing inch, gritting my teeth as she squeezed her inner muscles, gripping me so tight I nearly lost it. But I managed to get all the way in without blowing my load, and once we were one, I wrapped my arms around her and took a few seconds just to enjoy the feel of her.

Her fingers gripped my shirt on my shoulders, and her face was tucked into my neck. "I don't want this."

Her voice was soft in my ear, and I heard her internal struggle. But there was nothing to question. "You're MINE," I told her. "You'll always be mine, *amore*." With one arm under her ass and one hand protecting her head from the back of the door, I rolled my hips, pulling out of her slowly and then sinking back in, using the door to brace her. It felt so good. So *fucking* good. My eyes rolled to the back of my head as my hands tightened on her ass and hair.

Veda moaned, her arms wrapping around my neck. She made me feel strong. Powerful. Like I could do fucking anything as long as she was with me and I was inside of her.

"I have to fuck you." The warning was barely out of my mouth when I started to move, my hips jerking back and forth as I drove into her so hard she slammed up against the door with each stroke. I was worried I'd hurt her, but I couldn't speak, couldn't stop. My groin tightened sharply as my orgasm slid down my spine and into my balls. "I'm gonna come inside of you." My voice was rough. Breathless. "I have to come inside of you."

Her response was to tighten her legs and arms around me and hang on.

"Come with me, my *vita*. Come with me, *amore*." I adjusted my hips until I hit her clit with every thrust, and then I found the puckered hole of her ass with my finger and pressed.

"Oh my god!"

"Yes....come for me, *amore*," I gritted through my teeth, hanging on to my sanity by a thread as I slid my finger in. She was mine. Every fucking part of her.

"Luca!"

Ah, there it was. I locked my knees. With a shout I couldn't contain, my orgasm hit, pumping through me and into her in hot spurts as I pushed myself balls deep inside of her. I felt her come around me, squeezing my cock, the essence of us both joining together and becoming one. It was fucking real. And it was fucking right.

For a moment, all was peaceful in my world. I laid my forehead against hers and closed my eyes, my breathing ragged and my heart beating like it was going to break right out of my ribcage. *Stay with me.* I almost said it out loud. Words I shouldn't be saying. Just like I shouldn't feel the things I did. But fucking hell. How did I live without this woman? I didn't give a shit what she'd done. She was back in my arms. Where she belonged. No one else knew. And we could keep it that way. I could protect her.

A heartbeat passed. Two. *Fuck.* I was an idiot if I believed that. I tightened my hold on her, fighting with myself. I knew what I needed to do. But not yet. Not yet.

As if she could hear my thoughts, she suddenly went stiff. "Put me down," she ordered.

"And if I don't?"

"Luca. Put me the fuck down, or I'll scream this whole building down around us."

I pulled my head back so she could see the truth in my eyes. "No one would give a damn. And they wouldn't dare come in here even if they did." It was true, and she knew it. "So, go ahead, *amore.* Scream." My cock was still half hard and I rocked my hips, enjoying the way she inhaled on a hiss, her body swaying into mine as much as she tried to fight it.

A smile tugged at the corners of my mouth. "I can make it so you don't have a choice."

She stilled again, then shoved at my shoulders and tightened her legs around my hips, trying to lift herself off of my cock. "Fuck you, Luca."

"You just did. And you'll do it again."

"No, I won't."

Giving in, I lifted her away from me and stepped back, setting her feet on the floor. I opened the door, keeping her behind it, and found Enzo standing guard as I knew he would be. "Would you grab me a towel? And a shirt for Veda."

With a nod, he headed to the dressing room at the end of the hall and returned with a white towel and a black T-shirt with the name of the club sprawled across the front in neon letters. He wouldn't meet my eyes as I took it from him with a nod of thanks and shut the door, handing both to Veda.

As she turned away and cleaned herself up, I tucked myself into my pants. "If you want nothing to do with me, then why are you here, Veda? Why did you call me?"

She kept her back to me as she put on her panties and shorts and pulled her bra back up. Then she grabbed the shirt from the chair she'd dropped it in and tugged it over her head. "I didn't call you. I called Enzo."

"Which is calling me. So what happened?" I knew, of course. But I wanted her to tell me. To trust me.

"Nothing. It was nothing." A wave of utter disappointment surged through me as she ran her fingers through her hair. Her natural color was starting to come in. A much prettier blonde than her sister's bleached-out look. "I probably panicked over nothing." She turned to face me. "Are you going to stop me if I try to leave?"

Every cell in my body screamed *YES!* But I shook my head. "No."

My answer must've come as a surprise. She stared at me like she didn't believe me.

"You're free to go whenever you wish." I unlocked the door and stepped back, sitting on the edge of the desk and crossing my arms over my chest.

She took two steps toward the door and stopped. Over her shoulder, she asked, "Are you going to kill me, Luca?"

I didn't answer. I couldn't. "You need to get out of this city, *amore*. In time, Mario will figure out you're no longer with me."

Her eyes searched my face, looking for something she would never find. Always searching. And then she turned and walked out of the office.

I let her go.

CHAPTER 6
VEDA

$\mathcal{E}$nzo was outside the office, standing guard as he always did. I gave him the dirtiest look I could muster as I rushed past him.

"Veda! Wait."

I kept walking.

But he caught up to me easily. Laying a heavy hand on my shoulder, he spun me around before I even reached the end of the hallway. "Where are you going?"

"You knew he was here," I shouted over the music. I didn't care if Luca heard me or not. I felt raw. Exposed. Enzo had known he was in that office, and he'd sent me in there anyway. Did he know what Luca was going to do when I got here? Did he have any idea whether he would fuck me or shoot me the second I walked in? Did he even care?

"No," he said. "I didn't tell you."

"Why?"

"Because no matter what, my loyalty to you only extends as far as Luca."

Of course. I was stupid to think otherwise. To believe that all of the hours we'd spent together training and talking while I was at Luca's meant anything at all. I turned to leave without another word. I'd already embarrassed myself enough by looking like I came running over here for a booty call with the hot mafia guy who wanted to kill me. I was as stupid as Nicole if I believed anything different.

He grabbed my arm. "Where are you going?"

I yanked it free, and he let me go, but I made the mistake of glancing up at his face, and my anger deflated a bit. He might be loyal only to Luca, but there was general concern in the way he held his mouth. "I have to get my friend's car back."

He took off his sunglasses. "Veda, I don't think it's safe for you to be out by yourself."

A sad smile fluttered and died. "You're probably right. But is it really any safer for me to be here?"

His mouth thinned into a hard line as he studied me. "Hold on one second. Stay here. Okay?"

Heaving an impatient sigh, I nodded.

Enzo walked back to the office, knocked hard three times, and stuck his head in. After a quick conversation, he closed the door and came back to me. "I'll follow you back to your friend's. Make sure you get there okay and check out their place before I leave you."

"Thank you," I told him after a pause.

His hand on my lower back, he escorted me out of the club and to my car, putting his sunglasses back on that hid his eyes from me and everyone else before we'd even walked out of the club. "Where does your friend live?"

I hesitated only for a second before I gave him the address of Sammy's building.

"Okay. If anything happens and we get separated, you turn around and come right back here—"

I cut him off. "I can't do that."

"Veda, you'll be safe here. No matter what Luca says or doesn't say. He won't hurt you."

I laughed with no humor. "Oh, that's where you're wrong, Enzo. He already did."

"Veda. You know what I mean."

"But I don't know that I believe you."

He scanned the parking lot and the road and then came back to me. "I know Luca better than anyone, even Tristan. He couldn't kill you, Veda. I've never seen him like this with a woman. Not even his dead fiancée. To hurt you would be like killing himself."

I let him believe what he wanted to believe. "Fine. If we get separated, I'll do as you said."

He nodded his approval. "You come back here, and I'll go on to your friend's place and make sure she"—he raised one eyebrow, and waited for me to nod—"is okay."

"Sammy."

He gave me a questioning look.

"*Her* name is Sammy."

"I'll make sure Sammy is okay."

"Thank you," I told him sincerely.

The entire time we had this little conversation, I'd watched Enzo constantly scan the parking lot and street. "Alright. We need to go."

He put me in the car, standing nearby with his hand inside his jacket until I started the engine and locked the doors. Then he jogged over to the familiar SUV parked near a side door. I waited until he pulled up near me, and then we were off.

Enzo followed me all the way back to Sammy's apartments, and luckily, whoever had been tailing me earlier didn't make another appearance. Or maybe I'd overreacted and no one had been following me at all and I'd just freaked out over nothing, just like I'd told Luca.

I parked Sammy's car in her spot while the SUV idled behind me. When I got out of the car, so did Enzo.

Pointing up at Sammy's apartment where I could see lights on within, I said, "My friend is home. And it looks like one of her roommates is, too."

"I'm coming upstairs with you," he told me. "Just in case."

After a pause, I nodded. "Okay. I'd appreciate it."

I took him up to Sammy's and let myself in with the spare key she'd given me. Enzo followed me in as far as the living room. Taking off his sunglasses, he checked every corner, listening to Maddie having an animated conversation with someone in her room. Either she had a guest, or she was on FaceTime, but either way, everything seemed normal.

He turned to me. "What are your plans now?"

"I plan to say hi to Sammy and go to bed."

"No, that's not what I meant. What are you going to do with your life?"

Oh. That. "I don't know."

"You should listen to Luca and get out of town, Veda. Especially after what happened tonight."

I wasn't sure if he was talking about the car tailing me or my run-in with Luca. Hands on his hips, he stared down at me. Not for the first time, I noticed he had beautiful brown eyes, à la Johnny Depp. Eyes a girl could easily lose herself in. But they weren't intense blue glaciers that stripped me bare without touching me and set my blood on fire. "I promised my parents we'd do a memorial for Nicole. I have to stay for that so I can be there for them. And then I'll figure out where I'm gonna go." If my mother could stand to be around me that long.

"It would really be safer for you if you got out of town now. Tonight."

"Yeah, I'm not doing that. Not yet. I need to be there for my dad."

"Veda, please listen to me. To Luca. He wants you to be safe."

"If he cared at all, he wouldn't have chased me out of the fortress he lives in. But he did. And he wants nothing to do with me other than a quick fuck against his office door." My mouth twisted in disgust that was aimed only at myself. "He doesn't care about me, Enzo. He threw me to the wolves."

Done with this conversation, I started walking toward the door and he followed. "You're wrong, Veda. Luca is angry, and whatever your intentions were, he feels like you betrayed him. But I know him better than he knows himself sometimes. He won't come after you. So please, call if you need us. He'd never forgive me if anything happened to you, no matter what you think or what he says."

He stared at me so hard I finally gave in. "I promise," I told him. And I meant it. Despite the fact he'd sent me straight to Luca tonight, I knew Enzo was right. Alone, I was no match for a man like Mario. Or even one of his thugs. I didn't have the trust in Luca that Enzo had, but I knew he truly believed what he said. "Thanks again for making sure I got home."

He glanced around the kitchen and then back at me. "This isn't your home." Moving past me, he opened the door and walked out into the hallway.

Closing the door and locking it, I went to the window and watched until I saw him get into his car and pull away, trying not to think about his parting comment. I knew what he was insinuating, but it wasn't true.

No matter what I may have begun to secretly hope for once upon a time.

Double checking the locks on the front door, I went to go find Sammy. Maddie must've been on the phone earlier. I only heard the television in her room as I walked by.

I found my best friend sitting up in bed, her laptop on her legs with an open book beside her and a few more spread out on the bed. "Hey," I said.

She looked up. There was a pen between her teeth. She spit it out into her hand as soon as she saw me in the doorway. "Hey. How'd things go with the parents?"

"As expected." I decided not to tell her about my possible stalker. For one, I didn't want to worry her. And second, since they sped away, I didn't know for sure someone had actually been following me. Maybe it was just a strange coincidence, and I'd gotten all worked up over nothing.

"Did you get a new job?"

Distracted by my own thoughts, I plopped down on the bed beside her, crossing my ankles and grabbing a decorative pillow to hug. "Huh?"

"The shirt. That's a strip club."

I looked down, moving the pillow so I could see. I'd completely forgotten about the shirt. "Oh." I laughed. "No." Hoping she'd drop it, I asked, "Whatcha working on?"

She narrowed her eyes at me, and then blew out a breath and launched into a diatribe about how hard her Calculus class was and how she was going to have to spend the rest of her life in the tutoring lab if she wanted to have any chance at all of passing.

"I have faith in you," I told her.

She stared at me, and then she closed her laptop and set it aside, leaning back against the headboard. "You saw your hot gangster dude."

"What? No." I plucked at the corner of the pillow.

"Don't you lie to me, V. I know you did."

"Why the hell would you think that?"

"Because you smell like him. You smell like a man. A really good smelling man. And you smell like sex."

"Oh my god, Sammy. Stop!" I threw down the pillow and jumped off the bed.

She wasn't fazed by my dramatics. "It's true, isn't it?"

I swung around, my mouth open to deny it. But then I snapped it shut again. I sat down on the end of the bed, far away from her damn bloodhound nose. "Yeah. It's true."

"I thought you were at your parents'?"

"I was."

"Then how the hell did you end up fucking the guy who threatened to kill you?" She leaned over, eyeing my shirt again. "At a strip club, I take it."

I turned to face her. "I guess I should've told you this right away."

"Told me what?"

Holding up my hand to stop her questions before they started, I told her the truth. "I think someone followed me out of my parents' neighborhood."

"Followed how?"

"In a car. I was about to head back here when I noticed there was a black car behind me that seemed to come out of nowhere. I took a sudden turn, and it still followed me. So I freaked out and called E—" I caught myself just in time. Sammy was my best friend, and I'd known her most of my life, but the less she knew, the better. So, no names. "I called one of his men and he had me drive to the club. He met me outside, and the car kept going." I pulled my hair over one shoulder, too nervous to keep my hands still. "It might have been nothing. A coincidence. But I didn't know what else to do. And when I got there, *he* was there. And...things happened."

"Well, being that you came home in a different shirt you left in, I would say some very interesting things happened." Crossing her legs beneath her, she leaned forward. "But again. Why the hell didn't you just go to the cops?"

"I told you why."

She sighed heavily. "I just don't get why you're protecting this guy, Veda."

Yeah, well, that made two of us.

"It's not like you could ever have a life with him."

The truth, said out loud like that, hit me hard, and my voice was sullen when I said, "I never said I wanted one."

Sammy turned on the bed so she was facing me. She picked my hand up in hers. "V, I think it would be a good idea if you talked to someone."

I frowned. "I am. I'm talking to you."

She shook her head, her long braids cascading over her shoulders. "No. I mean like, professionally. I think you might be having feelings where you shouldn't. Through no fault of your own," she was quick to add.

I pulled my hand from hers. She was probably right. But that didn't mean I was going to do it. I'd be fine. I was fine. And my feelings weren't some consequence of emotional trauma.

"You've been through a lot of shit the last few months, and I just think it would be a good idea. I mean, the guy fucking kidnapped you, Veda. And you're over here all heart eyes for him. There's a name for that."

"Stockholm Syndrome," I answered flatly.

Quietly, she said, "I just think it might be a good idea. You know, when you get settled somewhere."

My eyes shot to hers. "Yeah," I told her after a pause. "I'll think about it."

Sammy gave me a small smile. "Good. That's good."

Getting up from the bed, I grabbed my pajamas and went into the bathroom to wash Luca's smell from me, ignoring the tears of loss that burned my eyes and mixed with the water from the shower.

CHAPTER 7
LUCA

"We got the information back from the license plates. It was one of Mario's men."

I swirled the whiskey around in my glass, concentrating on the way the glaring lights in the office touched the amber liquid. They hadn't seemed as harsh when Veda was the thing they adored.

Enzo was wasting energy running in here to tell me that. I didn't need proof. Who else would it have been? "I know."

He put his sunglasses on top of his head, pressed both palms into the desk, and leaned forward, his eyes hard on my face. "What are we going to do about it?"

"Nothing. I told her to leave town." I took a sip of my drink and leaned back in my chair, putting some space between us so I didn't dislocate his jaw. "If she doesn't, she has no one to blame but herself."

"So you fuck her and send her on her way to get killed?"

"I didn't bring her here. You did."

"Not so you could get your dick wet. I did it hoping you would quit being a fucking *stronzo* and pull your head out of your ass and *talk* to her."

I laughed. And even I heard the ugliness in it. "What the hell do you expect from me, Enzo?" I leaned forward, my laughter dying as quickly as it came on. "She fucking *betrayed* me. Tristan caught her digging around my office. Saw her with his own fucking eyes. What if she'd found something and reported back to Mario? And, for that matter, how do we know she didn't? She could've gotten me killed. Could've gotten all of us killed because of her lack of trust in me. Would you be so forgiving then?"

A muscle jumped in his jaw, but he didn't deny it. He couldn't. "Perhaps you haven't given her much reason to trust you."

I slammed my hands down on the desk. "What else could I have done?" I shouted.

He clenched his jaw, but he didn't push it.

I shoved my chair away and paced around my desk until I stood behind him, then waited for him to turn around. When he did, I gave him the truth. "I have to let her go, Enzo. For her safety as well as ours. You know it as well as I do. So don't you dare fucking stand there lording it over me. Remember who you work for."

His mouth twisted into something that in no way resembled a smile. "How could I forget?" he asked.

We stared at each other, and my fists clenched at my sides.

"And as to Veda, I don't know any such thing." He sat on the desk, his arms crossed over his wide chest. "You know as well as I do, she never would have done what she did if she'd felt like she had any other choice. Veda didn't grow up in this life. She's untarnished and easily manipulated. I shouldn't have to tell you that."

"What are you saying?" I asked him. "That you know her better than I do? You want her for yourself? Is that it?"

"Maybe she'd be better off."

A red haze clouded my vision, and with a roar of rage, my fist flew toward his face. He blocked me easily, but Enzo and I had been together for a long time. We'd trained together. I knew his tricks, and so I was prepared.

Ducking down and to the side, I brought my opposite fist up into his kidney, then grabbed his head with both hands and pulled his face into my knee.

He managed to turn his head enough that he avoided a broken nose, catching his sunglasses as they fell off his head. Hands together, he threaded them inside my arms, pushing them up and out, breaking the hold I had on his head.

We backed off, circling each other like animals. Enzo calmly folded up his sunglasses and set them on my desk, then unbuttoned his jacket. "Is this what we're doing, Luca? Huh?"

"I don't ever want to hear her name come out of your mouth again," I growled.

"You know damn well I would never disrespect Veda—or you—in that way. You're just looking for a fight because it's the only way you know to handle these things you feel for her."

"You don't know what you're fucking talking about."

He stopped moving. "Yes, my friend, I do. So why don't you stop being such a bastard. You don't owe anyone in this family anything. No one even knows what happened. Why are you putting her in danger because of your own fucked up sense of honor that they don't even deserve?"

I studied him for a moment. My friend. My brother. The man whose advice I respected above all others. A stabbing pain shot through my head, and I winced, rubbing my temples. He was right. I knew he was right. "Did you find out where she's staying?"

"I did." He said nothing else, and I knew he wouldn't until I asked him. I didn't want to know where my *vita* was hiding from me.

"Is she safe?"

He slowly shook his head. "No one followed us from here. I don't think he knows where she is. But he knows where her parents live."

My immediate reaction was to demand he take me to her. Or at the very least, go back and haul her gorgeous ass out of wherever the hell she was and bring her back to the lake house. But then I took a breath and concentrated on slowing my heart rate. "I'll send a few men over to watch her parents' place."

"Do you want to talk about this?"

"No," I told him. Then hesitated. "But I appreciate your honesty, even if it makes me want to bash your face in."

"Just think about what I said, Luca."

I nodded as the last of my rage cooled to the ever-present simmer that had been there since I'd told her to leave. Unable to help myself, I asked, "Did Veda say anything to you about what she planned to do?"

"She said she's staying until her family can hold a memorial and mourn her sister, and she'll figure out what she's going to do after that."

Jesus Christ. Why wouldn't she just go? Why was she tempting me like this? "She already mourned her sister. She stayed holed up in her room for weeks doing just that."

"But not with her parents. She needs this time with her family, Luca."

He was right. I knew this. But I couldn't stand the fact that she was putting herself in harm's way for something that wasn't absolutely necessary. From what she'd said, her sister was a bitch to her and treated her no better than a lowly servant. I don't know that I would show my father or my own brother the same respect when the time came. "She's a fool."

He picked up his sunglasses from my desk. "What do you want me to do?"

That was the question, wasn't it. I knew what I wanted, but I also knew that what I *wanted* to do and what I *needed* do to retain my position in the family were two very different things. "Nothing," I told him. "For now, do nothing. I'll send two of our men over to keep an eye on her parents' house. But that's it."

"Are you absolutely sure about this?"

No. I wasn't. But my hands were tied.

"Luca—"

Whatever he was about to say, I didn't want to hear it. "Call a meeting," I told him. "And get Tristan back here to report what he was able to find out about the other families. I want them all here at the club tomorrow night. We have a lot to do if I'm going to unseat my father from his throne."

He stared at me for a long moment, then picked up his sunglasses and put them back over his eyes. Pulling his cell from the inside pocket of his jacket, he started walking out of the office. "What time?"

"Nine."

With a terse nod, he left, closing the door behind him.

After he was gone, I went back to my chair and sank into it with a long sigh, staring at the numbers on the spreadsheet I'd been working on before Veda had come back to claw her way inside the open wound that housed my heart. But I might as well have been looking at a blank monitor screen, because I didn't see anything except her face. Didn't hear anything except her voice railing at me one second and moaning my name the next. And here, alone in this room, I could admit to myself what I refused to voice out loud to anyone else.

In the short time I'd known her, she'd become a part of my life. A part of me. And I fucking missed her more than I ever thought I could.

Closing the window on the computer screen, I rested my head in my hands and tugged at my hair. Enzo was upset with me. Hell, even Tristan didn't agree with the way I was handling things with Veda. Restless, I got up and refilled my whiskey.

I honestly didn't know how to get us out of the situation Veda had put us in when she was caught snooping around my office for my brother. According to the rules of the game that was my life—the only life I had ever known—I had no choice but to consider her a rat and dole out the appropriate punishment. Telling her to run was only a temporary reprieve. A wild chance that she'd run fast enough and far enough that I wouldn't be able to carry out what I knew I needed to do.

However, the thought of taking a gun and pointing it at her head made something clench inside of my gut, squeezing my lungs until I could barely breathe. I placed my hand in the middle of my chest, willing my heart to beat again. Her showing up here and walking back out alive was enough to send my father's words clanging around in my head. But he was wrong. I could do what needed to be done, if I had to, but I also knew her death would destroy me.

Life without Veda was a life I didn't want. I had no doubt that if I was forced to carry out my threat, I would do everything in my power to follow her into the black abyss as soon as possible.

The thought was appealing, if I were to be honest with myself. We'd be able to escape the problem of my father and brother and all of the stupid bullshit that came with them and be together wherever the fuck you go when this life was done.

The only problem with that plan was that I wasn't done with her luscious body in this world yet, and my physical craving for her far outweighed my desire to leave this fucked up world. Even now, not an hour after I'd had her, my body hardened at the thought of having her again.

I took another sip of my whiskey.

There had to be a way for me to keep her.

And the more I thought about it, the simpler the answer became. Enzo was right. No one other than Tristan, Enzo, and me knew what had happened. No one knew I'd forced her to leave. No one knew anything, not even my own men, and we could easily keep it that way.

So it was just a question of my honor.

I'd always prided myself on being a man who was in every way nothing at all like my father or my brother. I may be seen as cold and controlling by some, but I kept my word, and I always—*always*—conducted myself in an honorable way within the family. Being so close to taking my father's place, it would be a risk to let her get away with what she'd done. If anyone found out, I'd lose the trust of the other families, and I may very well end up in a grave myself for showing her mercy, something that was unheard of in my world unless you were in a position of ultimate power like my father. And my brother would rise in the ranks as intended unless someone was smart enough to kill him, too.

And Veda, my *vita*, would be left alone with the monsters.

I hadn't been thinking straight when I sent her away. Not once, but twice. She was on Mario's radar now, and as soon as he figured out she was no longer under my protection, she would be on everyone's. I'm sure word had gotten around by now as to who she really is and what she meant to me. She would never be able to live a life where they wouldn't find her. And she would be made even more valuable in their eyes because to take her would be one more way to twist the knife in my back, even if I was a corpse.

Enzo and Tristan would try to protect her, if for no other reason than out of their loyalty to me, but even as skilled as they are, they would only be able to run so far without the protection of the family. There was no way Veda would survive without my protection. And there was no *fucking* way I would be able to bring myself to kill her.

I slammed down the remainder of the whiskey and wiped my mouth on the back of my hand.

Honor be damned, her place was with me.

CHAPTER 8
VEDA

After two uneventful weeks, the day of my sister's memorial service arrived. I rode with Sammy to the funeral home, my hands twisted in my lap. I'd wanted to bring flowers, but with my allergies, it was impossible to have them in the car with me. I'd arrive looking like I just stepped out of a Rocky movie after the final match, so I'd sent them ahead.

My father had wanted to have the service at their house, but my mother talked him out of it. She said she didn't want the memory of mourning her daughter assaulting her every time she entered that room to watch television at night. And I was glad. Although Enzo had called me once to assure me they were under protective watch, and nothing else had happened, the chaos of people coming and going would make it too easy for someone to blend in with the crowd and slip inside my parents' home.

It was a huge relief that everyone I loved was safe and I'd had no reason to seek out the help of the man I was trying my damndest to forget, so why was I was so...restless?

With a sigh, I turned to look out the window. I knew why. Because I missed him. I missed Luca. More than I ever thought possible.

"How you doing, V?"

I turned to Sammy and gave her the best smile I could manage. "I'm okay. I'll be better when this is over."

She glanced over at me, her eyes falling to the dress I was wearing. "Well, you look too damn good in that dress to waste it on something so sad. If I didn't have to study later, and your life wasn't possibly in danger, I'd take you out for a night on the town when this was over."

I looked down at myself. The dress I'd found was simple and black, as befitted the situation, but even I had to admit it was a flattering style on me. It was sleeveless, but the neckline was high, cut straight across the bottom of my throat to cover the new scars on my chest. The bodice tapered down to my waist, where the skirt flared out in an A-line to my knees, hanging lower in the back. I wore low black heels on my feet and a simple silver chain. My hair was pulled back off my face, but left to tumble down my back in artful curls. Because I knew he liked my hair down. I'd also found a hair stylist that was able to match my natural blonde. For him. Because I knew he liked my natural color. Even though I shouldn't have spent the money. I even had a little bit of makeup on.

As if she could read my thoughts, Sammy asked, "Do you think he'll show up? Your hot gangster dude?"

I shook my head, even as hope flared in my heart. "No. Why would he?"

"To see *you*, Veda."

"He doesn't want anything to do with me."

"From the way you looked when you came home from the strip club that night, you'll understand if I disagree."

I turned to look out the window again so she wouldn't see the tears welling in my eyes. "And that was obviously a proper goodbye fuck, wasn't it? Because I haven't seen or heard from him since."

That came out sharper than I intended, but at least it got her off the topic of Luca. "Sorry," I mumbled.

She shrugged it off. "How's your mom been toward you since you've been back?"

"Oh, you know, the usual." My smile this time was bitter. "She blames me for Nicole getting mixed up with the wrong crowd. Blames me for not watching out for her better. Blames me for the fact that she died and not me..." I trailed off, looking down at my hands. "I don't know why I even bother."

"You do it for your dad."

She was right. "Yeah. I shudder to think what my life would've been like without him in it, having to deal with just my mom and my sister."

Sammy reached over and laid her hand over mine, stopping my nervous fidgeting. "Let's hope we don't ever find out, yeah? Because your mother is seriously fucked up, V." Giving me a squeeze, she returned her hand to the steering wheel and turned on her blinker to turn into the funeral home. "But if you do, you'll always have me. You're my family, V. You're all I have now."

"And I always will be," I told her, then leaned across the seat and gave her a kiss on the cheek.

She parked the car, and we gathered up our purses and got out of the car. "Ready?" she asked me.

"Not in the slightest."

"Great. Let's go." Linking her fingers with mine, we walked into the funeral home hand in hand to go say hello to my parents, holding our purses in front of our faces to avoid the photographers.

My sister was semi-famous, and now that word had gotten out about her death, people were crawling out of the woodwork to gawk at her grieving family and the few real friends she had. And my mother stood in the center of it all dressed in black lace and a veil, like the queen of the ball, accepting people's condolences while elegantly patting at her face with a tissue. It took everything I had not to roll my eyes. I knew she was grieving, but she could be sad and enjoy all of the attention at the same time. Actually, she was a pro at it.

Spotting my father sitting by himself in the front row of chairs, Sammy and I headed that way. "Hi, Dad."

He dragged his eyes away from the sight of my mother. "Hey, honey. Sammy. How are you?"

"I'm good, sir. Thank you."

He didn't even fuss at her for calling him sir. That's the only way I knew how upset he was. My father would be a badass poker player if he was a gambler. You rarely knew what he was thinking or feeling unless he told you.

I sat on one side of him, and Sammy sat on the other. Taking his hand in mine, I admired the large photo of Nicole that stood on a stand at the front of the room. Large flower arrangements surrounded it, and I felt a sneeze tickling my nose despite the allergy meds I'd taken before we left.

It was kind of surreal. The photo, the place, everything. But especially the photo. It was almost like looking at a picture of myself. Or at least the self I'd been forced to become while living with Luca.

The funeral director appeared in front of us to remind us there was coffee, tea, and water in the next room, along with some cookies and other snacks. My father thanked him, his eyes going to my mother as she sobbed in another woman's arms. The pain in his eyes was for her, for the way she was suffering, even though I knew he did, too. "Dad, can I get you a coffee or anything?"

"No, honey. Thank you." Tearing his eyes away from my mother, they went back to the large exposure of my sister's face.

"Okay. I'll be right back." Indicating to Sammy I was just getting a drink, I picked my way around the crowd surrounding my mother, accepting condolences and noticing a few looks of surprise when people saw my face.

Ignoring the stab of pain those looks caused, I found the ladies' room and shoved the door open, then locked it behind me.

It was stupid to feel this way. To be surprised that half of my mother's friends had no idea I existed. She'd treated me like this my entire life. Like an afterthought. One that came miles behind my sister and all of her many accomplishments.

I did my business and washed my hands, then wiped at my eyes, using the time to get myself together. Maybe it was just the rawness of my emotions causing me to be so sensitive to my mother right now. Because even though I'd known of my sister's death for weeks now, and I'd grieved her all alone, being here, in this place, with these people, made it all so real. Nicole was really gone. And I'd never see her again in this lifetime.

It was a sobering thought, and a lonely one, that I would face the rest of my life without my twin. And I felt guilty.

So, so fucking guilty. I'd wished for this very thing many times, never thinking it would actually happen. Well, not her death. But just that she would be out of my life. Yet, I thought she'd be here always, ganging up with our mother to make me miserable.

Tucking a tendril of hair that had escaped my hair clip back behind my ear, I took a bracing breath and opened the bathroom door. A quick glance toward my father assured me that Sammy was still sitting by him, so I made my way over to the table with the beverages.

I'd just finished stirring a little creamer into my coffee when a familiar voice said in my ear, "Hello, Veda."

Chills scattered across my skin, and my head jerked up. In the reflection of the mirror on the wall behind the table, Mario was staring at me, his eyes red and blotchy. My stomach tightened until I thought I was going to puke all over the cookies.

Oh my god. How long had he been here? My hand went to my bag to find my phone.

"I wouldn't do that."

Slowly, every cell in my body screaming in protest, I opened my fingers and dropped my phone back into my bag.

I watched in the mirror as his eyes went to my mother. Being here at my sister's memorial had obviously resurrected his grief, but seeing it from him stirred nothing inside of me. "You know, your mother is still a beautiful woman. I can see where you both got your looks. But your sister..." His eyes roamed up and down my mom. "Yeah...Nicole had her spark. It was just something inside of her, ya know?"

He looked to me as though for confirmation, but I kept my expression carefully blank. I knew what he was doing, and it wasn't going to work. I told myself he wouldn't be such a fool as to do anything that would bring undo attention to him. "What are you doing here?"

"I came to mourn my dead fiancée, of course." A slick smile teased the corners of his mouth. "And to see my second favorite sister." His smile fell. "I think we need to talk."

"No, we don't." My teeth began to ache, I was clenching my jaw so hard.

His eyes hardened, and he wrapped an arm around my back, his hand squeezing my hip painfully as he led me away from the table. To anyone who was watching, he appeared to be a concerned friend, a distant relative maybe, leading me outside to sneak a cigarette or just to get out of the crowd of people for a few minutes. I let him do it. The last thing I wanted to do was make a scene at my sister's memorial. My mother would never forgive me. She wouldn't care if I was in danger, as long as I didn't upset the last party she threw for Nicole.

But I wasn't a complete fool, and I dug in my heels when we reached the front lobby. No one was hanging out there, but there were plenty of people who would hear me if I so much as raised my voice. "I'm not going outside with you." There was no way in hell I was leaving the safety of this building.

When he saw he wouldn't be able to move me without making a scene, he acquiesced with a tight smile. "Fine. We'll talk here."

"There's nothing for us to discuss."

"No. There's not. There're only consequences. Because you haven't been living up to your end of the deal."

"There is no fucking deal." Not anymore.

One eyebrow went up, and I would've laughed at the surprised look on his face if I didn't think he'd pull out a gun and shoot me for it. Witnesses or no witnesses. "I'm going to go ahead and blame your sudden bout of amnesia on the fact that you're dealing with a lot right now. Ya know,"—he waved his hand around—"helping your sweet parents put together this lovely tribute to the woman who was going to be my wife."

"Until you killed her." I slammed my mouth shut. Surrounded by people or not, I knew better than to push him too far.

That slimy smile was back. "Do you want my precious brother to end up in a coffin at the front of that room?

Want your tears to be for him? Because I can make it so. It would solve one of my biggest problems, nice and easy."

He was right. It would. "So, why don't you just do that? Why go through all this bullshit?"

My response seemed to take him by surprise. "So anxious to have him out of your life already?"

"No," I assured him. Or maybe it was myself. "But it seems the easier thing to do. Or do you both just like fucking with innocent women?"

He watched my face for a few moments, studying me. Then he leaned in so close it was all I could do to stay where I was. "I'll let you in on a little secret, Veda," he finally said. "He doesn't deserve you. And I know he's putting the pieces in place to take over as boss, even if he has to off me to do it." He paused, and I saw a flash of something tender in his eyes. "But he's still my little brother. I want him gone, but I don't want him dead. Not if I can avoid it. And that's where you come in. All you need to do is give me something on him that will get him the fuck out of my hair, and you will save both my brother's life and my honor with the family."

Honor. It was all about their fucking honor. Everything they did. It was on the tip of my tongue to tell him that Luca kicked me out and he'd have to find himself another rat. But if I did that, he would know I wasn't under Luca's protection anymore. And he would have no reason to let me live knowing all that I know. "I can't get you anything," I told him instead. "He keeps everything locked up. I can't get access to it."

Leaning in until I could smell the coffee on his breath, he looked me dead in the eye. "Try harder."

"I *can't*."

"If you don't, I *will* kill him, though it will break my heart." He managed to pull off a regretful expression. "However, I'm giving you this chance to save him. And yourself." He tightened his grip on my arm, and his lips brushed my ear. "Get him out of my hair, and I'll allow him to live." Leaning back, his eyes dropped to the modest neckline of my dress. "But don't forget"—lifting his free hand, he traced the letter "M" over the scar on my chest with his fingertip—"you will always belong to me."

"If I were you, *brother*, I would step away from the lady. And I would do it right fucking now."

My head whipped toward the doors and my heart banged loudly in my chest as Mario stiffened, his grip on my arm tightening until I knew I was going to have bruises.

"Luca." His name on my lips was nothing less than an answered prayer.

Enzo and Tristan flanked him on either side, and I squeezed my eyes shut tight for a moment, never so happy to see the three of them as I was now. But my relief was short-lived when Mario's guys appeared from nowhere, trickling out of halls and doorways to surround our little party.

Luca appeared unconcerned by his brother's show of force. His blue eyes warmed only slightly when they turned to me. "I thought I would come and pay my respects, if that's alright."

CHAPTER 9
LUCA

The sight of my brother so close to her…

It took everything I had not to tear his fingers from her body and crush his skull between my bare hands. My blood burned in my veins and a red haze covered my vision, but I showed none of this. I held my body in perfect control, clenching my hands into fists in my pockets to restrain myself from wrapping them around his throat and squeezing until his lips turned blue and his eyes popped out of his head. "Step away from her. Slowly."

Instead of doing as I'd told him, Mario wrapped his arm around her waist and tugged her in closer. A flash of white-hot rage shot through me right before my heartbeat slowed to a heavy rhythm. My focus zeroed in on him. Did he know she was no longer under my protection?

"I believe you're outnumbered," he told me. "Rather careless of you to allow her to come here on her own." His men surrounded us, but I wasn't worried. They were idiots. Just like their boss. Enzo and Tristen could take half of them down before they even realized what was happening. "Would you really want to make a scene when I'm only here grieving with the woman who would've been my future sister-in-law? We've gotten rather...close...in the time we spent together."

Veda's face was ghostly white, and she was trembling so hard I could see it from where I stood, despite the determined set to her jaw and the cold fire flashing from her eyes. I knew if I gave her the indication to attack, she would do it without thinking twice. Before Mario could think to defend himself, I would be there to help her.

My brave girl.

But I decided to save that surprise for a time when it was needed more. "A scene? I'm not the one threatening an innocent woman in full view of a room full of people." I took a step forward and stopped. I had to force myself to keep my distance. To keep my voice down. "This is not the place nor the time for you to make your stand," I told my brother. "The nice people inside won't hesitate to call the cops, and not only will it land our asses in jail—at least temporarily—it will interrupt business and anger our father, just because you decided to have a pissing contest here and now. So step away from her, Mario, and we'll save this for another day when we won't be interrupted."

His upper lip lifted in a sneer and his bloodshot eyes darted from me to our men. I didn't have to turn around to know they all had their hands inside their jackets, resting on their guns. If he didn't back off, shots would be fired, and innocent people would get hurt. It was at that moment I realized, truly realized, how far gone my brother had become. "Mario, this is *not* the time."

His eyes shot back to me. And then he smiled. "You're right," he said. "I wouldn't want to be the reason Nicole's party was ruined." Something primeval bubbled up into my throat as he picked up Veda's hand, flipped it over, and kissed her palm. "Until we meet again."

"That's not going to happen," she ground out between clenched teeth, then she ripped her hand from his grasp and wiped it on her dress.

Mario just smiled. With an inconspicuous flick of his fingers, he told his men to stand down. Immediately, they fell in line behind him as he left the funeral home. At the door he turned. "Not very smart of you," he murmured. "Allowing her out in public alone like this."

I watched him go, giving Tristan a nod. Pulling out his cell phone, he followed Mario out of the building. He'd watch the cars leave and get the license plate numbers, so one of our men could follow him.

Veda stood where he'd left her, her wide, gray eyes now focused on me, just as watchful as before. Most of the tension had left the room with my brother. But now a different kind of energy filled the air between us.

I approached her cautiously, stopping when I noticed her spine stiffen. "You're not safe here."

Her eyes narrowed. "From whom, exactly? Mario? Or you."

I didn't respond to her question. I couldn't. Because I wasn't sure of the answer.

"Veda? You okay?"

A striking woman with dark skin and purple braids, wearing a stylish black pants suit, strode across the entry to her friend. Her large, brown eyes looked me up and down and obviously found me lacking. This must be Sammy, Veda's friend. If I wasn't so pissed off, my immediate impression would be that I liked her.

"I'm okay," Veda told her without taking her eyes from me. "Go back inside."

Sammy stared at me hard, then at Enzo. Tristan chose that moment to come back inside also, and her dark eyes shifted to him, then back to me. "Yeah, I don't think I will, V. I think I'm gonna keep my happy ass right here."

My smile felt tight. "I only came to pay my respects."

"The paying respects part is in there," she told me with a jerk of her head.

"Of course." I looked back at Enzo and Tristan and indicated for them to remain there by the doors, and then I made my way into the main room where Nicole's memorial was set up. Veda's parents stood together near a large photo of the woman I'd seen only once on TV, her face animated and her blue eyes sparkling with life. The photo was striking, obviously a head shot. Yet, still, there was something missing. Despite her bleached hair and bright eyes, she didn't have the vibrancy of her sister. Something that came from within, not from makeup and hair stylists and clothes. Veda could walk into a room in a T-shirt, jean shorts, and flip flops, and all eyes would turn to her. They wouldn't be able to help themselves. She was like the sun, pulsing warmth and life into everyone around her until all you wanted to do was get closer to her.

I didn't speak to her parents. In their grief, I knew I would seem cold. Uncaring. Because that's exactly what I was. I didn't grieve the death of their daughter. I was glad for it. If Nicole hadn't died, I wouldn't have gotten to know Veda.

She was nowhere to be found as I left the funeral home, my guts twisting as every instinct I had told me not to leave her there. But I couldn't very well throw her over my shoulder and walk out with her in front of all of these people. And now that her sister was properly laid to rest, she would try to leave. And if she succeeded, I might never see her again.

I couldn't let that happen.

"Let's go," I told the guys as I walked past them.

"What about Veda?" Enzo asked when we got outside.

"What about her?"

"We're just leaving her here? After what we just saw?"

"Yes."

Tristan stood in front of the door, blocking my way. "Luca, that's fucked up and you know it."

I did know it, but there was nothing I could fucking do about it at the moment, and that made me want to hit something. I narrowed my eyes at him as the blood rushed to my head. "Why do you continue to question me about her?" Frustrated with myself and everyone around me, I stepped into his personal space. Eye to eye, I smiled as he stilled. "Why does it matter so much to you?" I challenged.

His eyes darkened, and a muscle jumped in his jaw, clearly visible beneath his close-cut beard. I felt the tension grow between us. I fucking fed off it as I waited for him to throw the first punch. Because it couldn't be me. I would lose him forever if it was me. No one had to tell me that. Tristan was fucked up in a way I would never understand, which was perfect for this moment when my mood swung back and forth like a pendulum and a good fight would only give me an outlet for my rage. And his. The emotion a constant simmer just beneath the surface of his skin. But I couldn't strike first. Instinct told me he would never forgive me.

Enzo stepped between us, shoving his bulk between our bodies with his back to Tristan. "Jesus Christ. Back off, Luca. Right fucking now."

"Or what?" I asked him, without taking my eyes from Tristan.

Reaching up, he removed his sunglasses. "You don't want to do this. Not now. Not with Tris. If you're still itching for a fight, you can take it out on me."

He was right. I knew this. And yet, I couldn't force my feet to move.

Enzo knew me better than anyone. "Tristan, why don't you go get the car? Tristan!"

With a jerk, his eyes shifted to Enzo's profile. He gave a nod, turned, and walked outside.

Enzo gave me a shove, forcing me back. I wiped the back of my hand across my mouth and fixed my coat.

"What the fuck is your problem, Luca?"

That was a good question.

"Luca!"

I shoved past him as Tristan pulled the car around to the front of the funeral home, Enzo hot on my heels. He didn't say anything else. Not until we got into the car.

Then he turned around in his seat to give me a hard stare. "What the hell is the matter with you?"

"Take us home, Tristan," I ordered, ignoring him.

"I asked you a fucking question, Luca. We've known each other a long time, and I've never been anything but loyal to you, but if you think I'm going to stick around when you can't even keep your shit together—"

"You don't need to worry about me," I told him.

He shook his head, turning to fasten his seat belt when the SUV wouldn't stop chiming. "Don't turn into your father," he said quietly.

I turned to look out the window. He was right. He was fucking right, and I knew it. "I apologize, Tris," I told him.

He glanced at me in the rearview mirror but said nothing.

"Fuck." I scrubbed my face with my hands.

"It's alright," Tristan said.

"No, it's not alright," Enzo countered, turning back around to point a finger at me. "It's not fucking alright at all. You need to burn off some steam? Fine. We do it in the fucking gym. You don't turn on the only two friends you fucking have."

Enough with this shit. "Are you forgetting who you work for?" I asked him.

He didn't even blink at my cold tone. "Are you forgetting who keeps your ass alive?"

His words hit me like a bucket of ice. "No," I said after a pause. "No. I haven't forgotten."

Satisfied, he turned back around in his seat. "I love you, Luca. You know that. I love you like a brother. But you ever go after Tristan like that again—"

"I don't need you to protect me," Tristan told him quietly.

Enzo glanced over at him. "Yeah, I know you don't. But I will. Just like I protect that asshole back there." He pointed his thumb toward the back seat. He turned around again. "And I always will."

I held his stare until he turned back around.

They were quiet after that, leaving me alone with my thoughts. When we got to the house, I asked Tristan to come to my office with me. Alone.

"I am sorry," I told him. "I shouldn't have done that. I don't even fucking know why I did."

He walked over to the side table and poured us both a drink. "Because you're feeling a lot of things you're not used to, and you don't know how to process those feelings. And it makes you angry. It makes you feel out of control. So you do something that will make you feel in control again. Usually something *stupido*."

I took the drink from him, staring down at the amber liquid as I swirled it around in my glass. "Is there another way to fix that?"

"Yeah." He took a sip of his drink. "Stop fucking feeling things."

"I wish it were that easy."

His eyes went to the window, and he stared out at the bright, sunny day. "So do I," he said.

CHAPTER 10
VEDA

I barely held it together as I watched Luca walk out of the funeral home, Enzo and Tristan on his heels. As soon as he was gone, I made my way through the crowd of mourners, most of whom never even knew my sister but were only there for a photo op with a famous person. Even a dead one.

I was shaking, and tears I couldn't contain leaked from my eyes to trail down my cheeks. I guess if you're going to cry in public, a memorial for your twin sister is the place to do it. No one questioned me about my tears, or for avoiding them as I rushed past. They just looked on with similar expressions of pity.

When I reached the bathroom, I slammed my palms into the door to open it and rushed inside. In the center of the room I stopped, then spun around to look at the door again. I didn't know where to go or what to do. I just knew I couldn't be near other people right now.

Sammy followed me in, closing the door and locking it behind her. She leaned her back against it, stuffed her hands in the pockets of her dress slacks, and eyed me. One eyebrow went up. "I take it that was the guy you've been fucking these past few weeks."

I nodded as a sob erupted from my throat before I could stop it. Slapping my hand over my mouth, I took a few deep breaths through my nose. There was no way I could describe to her that being with Luca was so much more than just "fucking." It wasn't even love. It was intense. Consuming. And terrifying. And it twisted me up inside until I couldn't decide if I wanted to stab him in his sleep or chain myself to him so he'd never be able to leave me.

So many emotions crowded inside of me I couldn't differentiate between them. They shoved and pushed and ripped and expanded until I felt like I was about to explode, but I was afraid if I let it happen, I'd break apart into so many pieces I'd never be able to fit them all back together again. So I stood there, staring at my best friend with one hand holding in my screams and the other pressed against my stomach in an effort to hold myself together.

Sammy didn't try to come any closer to me. She'd been my friend long enough to know how fragile I was right now. She didn't ask me about Mario, and I could only assume she hadn't seen him take me out into the lobby. Thank god. Because I didn't think I'd be able to keep it together if she asked me who he was, or if she'd overheard anything he'd said. *Especially* if she'd overheard anything he said.

"What was he doing here?" she asked.

My hand still over my mouth, I shook my head. I honestly didn't know.

"What did he say?"

I stared at my friend, borrowing from her calm strength until I thought I could speak. Carefully, I lowered the hand that was covering my mouth and placed it on my stomach with my other one. "He said he came to pay his respects."

"Yeah, I heard that part. What did he say before that?"

"Nothing," I said, and the lie was sour on my tongue. "You came in right after he did."

She didn't believe me. I could tell she didn't. But she let it go. "What do you need from me?" she quietly asked.

I tried for a smile and failed. "Just...just stay here with me until I can go back out there."

"You got it." Adjusting her stance into a more comfortable position, she glanced around the bathroom. "Good god, this place is gaudy."

I looked around. She was right. It was all white and black marble, with veins of gold. The floor, the sink, the panels on the walls. And not to be outdone, the faucet and even the handle on the toilet were bright gold. "Yeah, it is." But Sammy wasn't looking at the decor anymore. She was looking at me. "I have to get away from him," I whispered.

"Yeah," she said. "I think you do."

Tears filled my eyes and escaped to run down my cheeks and my voice was barely audible when I confessed, "It hurts, Sammy."

She closed the space between us and wrapped her arms around me. "I know, V. I know."

Gradually, I felt the tightness in my chest began to relax. But we stayed in there, making idle comments about the funeral home, the people, and any other nonsense we could think of, until someone knocked on the door.

"You okay?" Sammy asked me.

I took a breath. Nodded. "I think so." As I walked over to the sink to rinse my face, she yelled that we'd be out in a minute. Then she reached out her hand and I took it. She squeezed tight, and together, we went back out to face my parents.

Four days later, I was with Sammy in her bedroom. She watched me from the bed as I closed the suitcase she'd given me the day before. I'd spent the time since Nicole's memorial saying goodbye to my parents, closing my bank account, and trying my damndest not to think about why I was leaving. Because every time I did, that twisty ball of emotions I'd shoved down inside of me with nothing but sheer force of will would threaten to overflow, and I'd have to hurry and distract myself before I ended up on the floor on the verge of a nervous breakdown.

I'd swapped out my cell phone again and given my dad my new number, but made sure he understood he was only to call for life or death emergencies. Otherwise, I would contact them when I felt it was safe for all of us. I also gave it to Sammy with the same instructions, and told them both they were not to give it to anyone else, no matter what.

"Are you sure you don't just wanna go to the cops?" Sammy leaned forward away from the headboard and wrapped her arms around her drawn-up knees, her expression tense with worry. "I don't want you to go, V."

"It's not safe for me to stay here any longer," I told her. "They'll find me eventually, and when that happens, they'll find you, too." I looked up to see her staring off toward the wall. I sighed. "It's just until things calm down and I'm forgotten about."

She huffed out a laugh, but there was no humor in it. "The way that man was looking at you at the memorial? He's not gonna be forgetting about you anytime soon. If ever. And I think you're stupid if you think otherwise. That dude is completely obsessed with you, Veda.

Honestly, the vibes I get from him are a little bit scary. And not completely because of what he does for a living."

Leave it to Sammy to say things exactly the way she sees them. "I think you're exaggerating."

"No," she told me in all seriousness. "I don't think I am. And it scares me."

I heard the weight in her tone and stopped looking around for anything I might have forgotten to pack. Her mouth was pressed together, and there were tight lines of worry around her eyes. "He'll forget me when I'm gone," I assured her. "The game is over. And the next one will have different players and he won't even remember my name."

"I don't think so," she argued. "I don't know who that guy is, because you won't tell me,"—she raised that eyebrow again—"but he looks like a man who likes to win. And I don't see him giving up that easily."

"I'm not a prize, Sammy. I'm a person."

"I'd bet my left tit you're *his* prize. The only one he wants."

I stared at her for a moment. She'd lost her ever-loving mind. Ignoring the twinge of unease and—dare I admit it, even to myself?—hope caused by her observation, I grabbed my suitcase and pulled it off the bed. "You're being ridiculous. He kicked me out of his house."

"I'm just worried about you. I don't think he's going to let you run away."

"Well, he has no idea I am, so he can't stop me." I looked around one last time. "Ready? I have a bus to catch."

She looked like she wanted to say more, but in the end, she just said, "Yeah," and got up to join me at the door. "I'm gonna miss you."

"I'm gonna miss you, too." Tears filled my eyes and I blinked them away as I hugged her. Angry tears. Fuck Luca and his psychotic brother. If it wasn't for them, my sister would be alive, and I would still be the girl I was before I'd met them. Not this scarred woman who was about to run for her life. Alone.

And yet, the more I hated him, the more I longed to run back to him and beg him to forgive me. I missed the feeling of safety I felt in his arms when he held me tight against him all through the night. The way my body would begin to burn from nothing more than a look. The way he pushed me. He made me feel more like a woman than any man I'd ever known. And yet, somehow, amidst the helplessness of being his captive, I'd emerged stronger than I ever was before. Powerful. Without him, I felt sad and small and weak.

I shoved away the thought as we made our way down to Sammy's car. I told myself I didn't want him. My body did. And it would be fine once I found someone else who would give it some attention. What was the saying? The best way to get over a man was to get underneath a new one?

And if I believed that, I was a fool. But was trying my hardest.

We made it to the bus station and Sammy came in with me while I waited. She ran her eyes up and down my frame, eyeballing my yoga pants and favorite sunflower tee. "You gonna be warm enough?"

"Yeah. I've got a hoodie in my carryon, and I'll get a heavier coat when I get where I'm going."

"Remember to let me know where you end up as soon as you can."

"I will."

"And call me from a pay phone and hang up when I answer at every stop, so I know you're safe."

"I don't think pay phones exist anymore."

"Then call from any phone except your cell phone. Borrow somebody else's phone. You know, so they can't track you."

I laughed, but it quickly faded away. "Okay. I promise."

The announcer came over the speakers, telling us my bus had arrived. I planned to go north to Montana and then...I had no idea. I just wanted to get as far from Texas as I could get before I stopped. I had my passport. Maybe I'd keep going into Canada until I thought it was safe to leave the continent. After all, I'd always wanted to go overseas.

I stood up, and Sammy did the same, grabbing me in a bear hug. "I mean it. Call me as soon as you can."

I hugged her back and tried to reassure her. "It'll be okay, Sammy. You'll see. I'm gonna find someplace gorgeous and then you can come visit me. Soon."

She nodded, but didn't seem convinced. "I'll wait here until the bus leaves."

"Okay." Kissing her on the cheek, I pulled up the handle of my suitcase and rolled it outside to where the bus was loading its passengers. As I waited in line, I didn't look back. I was afraid if I did, I wouldn't go through with this. And I had to leave. If not for my own safety, then for the safety of my friend and what was left of my family. I didn't even try to keep my departure a huge secret, although I didn't tell Sammy that. I put the ticket in my name and paid with a credit card. My hope was that I would lure Mario and his goons away. They'd follow me, and my parents would be safe until I could figure out how to get them out of town.

The bus driver loaded my suitcase into the storage compartment underneath the bus and I made my way over to the door to get on. I'd just found a seat near the front when my phone rang. One glance at the screen and my heart began to pound so hard my vision went blurry for a second. I tried to calm myself. I told myself there were any number of reasons he could be calling. But inside, I knew I was full of shit. I was too late.

My heart in my throat, I accepted the call. "Dad? What's wrong?"

"Veda?"

He sounded strange, like his tonsils were too large for his throat. "Daddy, what's happened? Are you okay?"

When he finally responded, he could barely get the words out. "Your mom and I...we're at the hospital...some men broke into our house last night. I tried to fight them...to keep them off her..." His voice trailed off, and I heard him fighting not to break down. "Your mother...they...oh, god..."

I stood up from my seat and started making my way off the bus against the flow of loading passengers. "I'm coming," I told him. "I'm coming! Where are you? Dad! Where are you?"

He gave me the name of the hospital and I hung up after assuring him I'd be there as soon as I could. Then I got my suitcase back and ran toward the station.

Sammy must've seen me coming and met me outside, grabbing me by the shoulders to stop me from running right past her. "Veda! What are you doing?"

"He went after my parents," I told her. "I have to get to the hospital."

Even though there were a million questions in her eyes, she didn't ask them. Instead, she pulled out her car keys and led the way back to her car.

"Can you drive any faster?" I asked her when we were on the highway.

"Why would he do that? Why would he go after your parents?"

I knew she was talking about Luca. "It wasn't L...him. It was his brother. The one who was engaged to Nicole." I paused, my throat closing up. "This is my fault, Sammy. Because I didn't do what he wanted me to do."

She reached over and took my hand. "This isn't your fault. And do you know that for sure? That it was him?"

"Who else would it be?"

"A random break-in?"

But I knew in my bones there was nothing random about this. Mario had done this to get my attention. He couldn't get to Luca, or me, for that matter, since he thought I was still there, so he went after my parents. And I was stupid to think that I could keep them safe by leaving first. That he would forget about his threats to me.

And then I thought of something else. What if he was waiting for me at the hospital? What if this was all a trap? A way to get to me?

Digging around for my phone, I found it in my back pocket. With shaking hands, I punched in Enzo's number.

"Who are you calling?" Sammy asked.

"The only ones who are capable of dealing with this."

CHAPTER 11
LUCA

My father never failed to make an entrance, especially when he had a full room of people to show off in front of. The power he wielded as the boss of this family had always been too much for him. He continually felt the need to exploit it. And although he normally listened enough to those around him in order to be somewhat logical when it came to decisions about the family business, over the years that need to be reassured of his power and importance had begun to sway his arguments. But he was the boss. And when he gave us orders, no one dared to contradict him for fear they wouldn't wake up the next morning, because he also didn't put up with disobedience. When he made mistakes, the rest of us did as he commanded without question, even knowing we were about to get fucked. It was important to respect the position, if not the man.

But not this time. This time, I would go down fighting.

I stood up from my chair, buttoning my jacket as I turned to face those seated behind me, and met the eyes of every man in the room. We were gathered in my father's office for a private meeting. Only those men in a top position of power in the family were here. They would make sure the word spread about the decisions made and that my father's orders were carried out exactly as told.

However, today I saw sympathy in the eyes looking back at me. Understanding. Rebellion. Hatred. I'd spoken with all of them before this meeting, unbeknownst to my father, and they were all familiar with my father's inclinations toward Mario.

I turned back to the man seated like a king behind his oversized desk. Mario, my brother, and the man who had just been officially named as my father's successor, was suspiciously missing from this very important meeting. He was no longer in hiding, and if there was anyone who didn't realize he was back, they would know after today, so there was no reason for him not to be here. It made me uneasy.

"I beg you to rethink this decision," I told him, careful to keep the anger out of my tone. "Mario isn't fit to run this business. He doesn't care about our family. Only about his own gains."

"He is my eldest son," Luigi bit out. "It is his right."

"He is out of his fucking mind, *padre*," I told my father for the hundredth time, hoping somehow, in front of witness who will agree with me, it might actually get through to him. "And he'll drive the business into the ground and all of us into an early grave."

This meeting had been called a week ago to discuss the anointment of the next boss. Someone who normally works closely with the current head of the business in preparation to take over. The families would witness it, agreements would be made, and this way, there would be no fighting when it came time. It would be a smooth transition.

The only problem was, that someone was me, not my brother. Mario had been completely out of contact with the family these last three years. And I couldn't sit here and say nothing. Not when my own honor was at stake. I'd given up everything for this family. I was never asked what I wanted to do with my life. No one cared. I'd given up any aspirations I might've had to do something else with my life for the business. And on the way, I'd lost people who were important to me. Friends. Maria. And now I could lose Veda. We would never be able to have a life together as long as Mario was still alive.

"He is not fit to take your place. You have to see this." I waved my arm toward the back of the room. "There are others here who agree with me. Just ask them." Over the past week leading up to this meeting, I'd been in contact with nearly every man in this room. They'd all agreed to back me up. They knew Mario. Knew he wasn't stable and that he'd ratted us out the day he took Maria's life and brought the feds into the mix. And then he'd cowered behind their protection until the dust had settled and he'd had a chance to get to our father and fill his ears with lies.

My father sighed heavily and turned his eyes to the rest of the room, as though he were patronizing a small child. "Who here agrees with Luca on this? Eh? Gino? What do you say about this?"

I found the man I'd met on the lake that day with Veda sitting near the back of the room, but he wouldn't meet my eyes. "I'm good with whatever you decide, Luigi," he said.

"Are you fucking kidding me?" The words were out of my mouth before I could stop them. "What the fuck, Gino? We had an understanding."

The big man shrugged. "Sorry, Luca. But I gotta take care of my own."

Which meant my father had gotten to him after our agreement was made and probably threatened to cut off the legs of his sons if he sided with me.

Son of a bitch.

Looking around, I knew without asking that he'd gotten to the rest of them too. The bastard was one step ahead of me, as always. "No." I shook my head. "No." All eyes turned to me. "Mario killed a woman I loved. Shot her in the head while my cock was still inside of her because he felt threatened by me and my success in the business." Most of those in the room knew what happened, but I could tell by the shocked expressions there were a few who had never heard the details. "She was an important member of the cartel and I worked with her and her brother for a good year before Mario fucked it all up by killing her. If it wasn't for the fact that her brother and I had a mutual respect for each other, we would've had a war on our hands. He brought the feds in to bust up the transaction, and then he hid in witness protection like the fucking coward he is. But that wasn't enough for him. Now that he's back, he's filled our father's ears with lies. Lies about me." I pointed to the center of my chest. "He still has it out for me because I know who he really is. I don't believe his lies. I'm not fooled by the charm that oozes from his pores. It's all a facade to hide the piece of shit he really is."

There were murmurs among those in the room.

"But my personal relationship with my brother aside, Mario is a rat," I continued. "And he needs to be dealt with accordingly." I saw a few nods. "My father, understandably, doesn't have the balls to do what needs to be done."

"Watch your fucking mouth, boy."

I gave him a nod of apology. "I'm sorry, *padre*. But it's true. You know the kind of man Mario is. You know what he did. You're not stupid. And yet, you let him get away with whatever the fuck he wants to." I held his eyes with mine.

"You always have. You've created a monster. And now it needs to get put down to protect the rest of us."

Pure fury held him stiff as he stared me down. I wasn't afraid, although maybe I should've been. "You have no idea what you're talking about. Your brother has done nothing but act on orders, MY orders, all these years. He's a good boy. Loyal. And he never questions me the way you do."

Ah. So that's what this was all about. I shook my head as the truth slowly dawned on me. "You want him to take your place so you can still rule the family through him. Because Mario would lick the piss off your balls if you told him to." It all made sense now. Again, I faced the men in the room. "You heard what my father said. This isn't right. Our family is better than this. Mario is a rat. And we have a code of honor to uphold. You all know what needs to be done. We were lucky the last time. Mario's goal was only to fuck with me. To bring me down a peg or two. But what if it's you next time? What if it's your son or your daughter he decides needs to be taken out? If he becomes the boss of this family, what will you be able to do?" I paused to let that sink in. "I'm not doing this to try to worm my way into my father's position. If any of you think someone else would be a better boss for this family, then that's fine. I would be more than happy to step aside, give them my loyalty, and continue on as the Underboss."

I heard more mumbling. They all knew there was no one else who was as prepared as I was to lead this family and our business. I felt the heat of my father's glare, but I refused to look at him.

Gino stood up. "Luigi, my friend, maybe we should listen to Luca and discuss this matter further before we make a decision."

But my father slammed his hand down on the desk, bringing an instant silence to the room. "There will be no more discussion. My decision is made. Mario is not this person Luca tries to make him out to be. He's a good boy. He does what he's told. And he's smart enough to understand there can be no discord within the family. That woman that Luca was fucking, she would've torn our family in two. Mario did you all a favor when he shot her."

"What the fuck are you talking about?" I asked him. The man was insane. "Marrying Maria would have only made our relationship with the cartel stronger."

"We have to have trust," he continued, completely disregarding what I'd said. "And you"—he pointed his finger at me—"you will sit down. And shut up. And stop this stupid vendetta with your brother."

"There are codes we live by, *padre*, and we have those codes for a reason."

"SIT DOWN!"

I snapped my jaw shut and faced off with my father. Taking this any further would only fuel his argument that I was unsuited for the position of boss. I needed to remain calm. Rational. Already I could see a few of the others giving me looks.

I unbuttoned my suit jacket and sat down.

Luigi got up and came around his desk. Two of my cousins, who were his constant bodyguards, came into the room as though on cue to stand beside and slightly behind him. Although they appeared relaxed, not one of us was fooled. They were there as a warning. My father was done with any discussions. This meeting was down to whatever he decided. And anyone who disagreed would do so at the risk of being shot down where he stood.

He met the eyes of everyone in the room one by one, saving me for last. He didn't look away as said, "My son, Mario, is under my protection. He is next in line to be boss. If there is anyone here who doesn't agree with my decision, I don't give a fuck. If anyone here brings any harm to him...*anyone*..." Again, his eyes bore into mine. "I will not hesitate to take the necessary measures to rid myself of that person who dares to bring dishonor upon me and my family." Looking around the room, he asked, "Any questions?"

There was only silence. We all knew better than to speak when he was like this.

"Good. Now get the fuck out of my house." He didn't look at me again as everyone rose and began to file out of the room to go home to their wives and children.

My blood boiled, and as much as I longed to rage my displeasure, I did the same. Our private conversations were one thing, but by making this proclamation here, in front of everyone, my father had basically just cut off my balls. His message was clear:

If I kill Mario, I'll be lying in the grave beside him within twenty-four hours.

Enzo was waiting for me by the front door. "We have a problem," he told me quietly as he held the door for me.

My heart stopped beating, then picked up again, pounding so fast and hard I felt lightheaded. I started walking, and he followed me. "Veda?"

He shook his head. "She's fine, as far as I know. I just got off the phone with her. It's her parents. Both are in the hospital, and Veda is on her way there now. It appears your brother wanted to send her a message."

I stopped walking and spun around. "She can't go there."

"I know. What do you want to do?"

I didn't even hesitate. Here was the opportunity I've been waiting for. "Send Tristan and two others to the hospital to get her parents and bring them back to the house. Then let Veda know where they are. Drop me off at the house so I'll be there to greet them, and then you can meet her near the marina and bring her back with you."

He was on the phone before I finished speaking.

As we got into the car, I tried to think of what I could say to her that would convince her to stay. My father had just taken away the only chance I had of allowing her a normal life, safe from my brother, and away from me. Not that I'd ever intended to give her that. I realized now, when I'd told her to run, that I'd always intended to find her again...after I'd killed Mario.

But killing him was no longer an option. Now I didn't have to wait to bring her back. And bringing her parents to my house was the perfect move.

CHAPTER 12
LUCA

Having Veda's parents safely ensconced in my home was...interesting. Even in the horrendous condition they were in, I could see almost immediately where the sisters had gotten their different personalities. Nicole, from the way Veda had described her, must have been the spitting image of her bitch of a mother.

The father, on the other hand, was a little harder to read. However, he'd just been beaten to within an inch of his life trying to protect his wife, so I had to respect him somewhat for that. Being attacked in the middle of the night wasn't a normal thing for him, and he'd done the best he could to protect the two of them. It also made me see where Veda had gotten her inner strength and integrity from.

As soon as Enzo got back on the phone with Veda, he'd told her to stay where she was until she heard back from him. Tristan rushed to the hospital under my orders. With a little "persuasion," he'd managed to get her mother released sooner than her doctor would've liked, as she was in much worse condition than her father, who'd already been released, but remained by his wife's side.

My brother, expecting me to be at my father's meeting, only had one man watching for Veda, and he was easily surprised and disposed of. And now I knew why he wasn't at the meeting to determine his future. Then I had her parents brought here to the lake house. Security had been doubled, and no one was allowed to come or go from the property without reporting to me.

Now, in my office with Enzo and Tristan, I half wondered if I'd lost my fucking mind by bringing her parents here. Or if it was the most sane idea I'd had since I'd met her.

"Call Veda and tell her her parents are safe," I told Enzo. "And that she has my word they will remain that way as long as they are here. If she wants to see them, she'll have to come to me."

"What are you doing, Luca?" Tristan asked.

I purposefully avoided what I knew he was truly asking. "I don't think my brother has a hard-on for her parents. He did it to get her attention. Or mine. And as far as we all know, he's not aware she hasn't been here with me, so having them in my safekeeping will make sense to him. And will piss him off." It gave me pleasure to think of

Mario as frustrated as I felt at the moment. "And it will also bring Veda back to me. To us," I corrected.

"So, you're using her family to get to her." His voice was hard.

My eyes shot to his and his eyebrows rose in silent question. "Yes," I told him honestly, then turned away. I didn't need another lecture right now. "Enzo."

With a nod, he pulled out his cell to do as I'd ordered, putting the call on speaker.

I walked over to the window behind my desk, trying to ignore the way my stomach jumped when I heard her voice on the line. She sounded so scared. I wanted nothing more than to hold her against me and soothe those fears.

Enzo related the news to her that her parents were safe and in my house. She did not sound happy about this good news.

"Put Luca on the phone."

I held out my hand to take the phone and took it off of speaker, before holding it up to my ear. She didn't even give me a chance to say hello.

"What are you doing?"

"Why does everyone keep asking me that?" I mused aloud.

"Goddammit, Luca. What are you doing with my parents?"

"They are safe," I told her.

"In your house? No. No, they are not. Give them back to me, Luca!"

"You called us," I reminded her. "What did you think I was going to do?"

She cursed again, and I heard her friend asking her what was going on. Veda told her, "He *took* my parents."

"Veda, you're being ridiculous. Your family is safe. I did what you wanted. I don't understand why you're so upset with me."

Her voice rose. "Why I'm upset? You weren't supposed to *kidnap* my parents, Luca! Just protect them!"

"I am protecting them, *amore*. Don't you see? Mario wants you distracted, so you'll mess up and he'll be able to get to you. The safest thing for all of you is to be here. I can keep you all safe."

"That's not going to happen," she told me. "Have Enzo meet me somewhere. I can take them with me back to the hospital."

"No," I growled.

"Oh, goddamnit, Luca, I'm not playing this game with you."

"I assure you, *amore*, this is no game. Your parents, and your mother in particular, are in no condition to leave. My physician is on his way."

I looked over to Enzo and Tristan and pointed my chin at the door. They stood up from their chairs and left me alone in the office, closing the door behind them.

"Luca?"

"Come back to me," I told her. "Tell me where you are and I will come get you. Most of your stuff is still here and I'll buy you whatever else you need."

There was only silence on her end.

"Veda..."

"I can't do that," she said quietly.

"I miss you," I admitted. "And you belong here. With me."

"Maybe you should've thought of that before you kicked me out of your house and told me to leave town."

I thought about my words carefully. "I was angry. I thought you had betrayed me."

She hesitated only for a moment before she asked, "And what do you think now?"

The lie was on the tip of my tongue. But in the end, I went with the truth. "I don't know what to think. And I don't care. I just want you here, where you belong."

She was silent again for a long time. And when she finally spoke, I could hear the tears in her voice. "And that's exactly why I can't come back."

I heard her friend talking to her in the background. She didn't appear to be a fan of mine. I needed to get her alone, where no one else was in her head but me. "Veda, please. I can send Enzo to get you, if you'd prefer, and we can talk."

"I just want to see my parents," she said. "That's all."

"I will bring you here to see them. If you promise me, you'll talk to me afterwards." I wasn't a complete bastard.

"No, I can't do that."

"Can't, or won't?"

"Do not underestimate me, Luca," she said, and there was a tone of fortitude in her voice I hadn't heard before. "You got super comfortable with me the last few weeks I was there. I know you're only about a mile from the marina. And I know what direction. I could find your house. Quite easily, I think."

"You'll never make it inside unless I tell my men to let you in," I insisted. "Also, my brother had a man at the hospital. He's watching for you, Veda. If you come here, you could bring him straight to me, putting all of us in danger. Including your parents."

"No one is following us."

I heard her giving directions to Sammy. "VE-DA, do not be stupid. You will bring him right to my door."

"That's not my problem," she told me. "Maybe you should've thought about that before you stole my family from me."

"Goddammit! I did not fucking steal them!"

She was silent for a long moment, then softly said, "Liar."

"Despite what you may think of me, I'm not a complete monster. I brought your parents here so they would be safe."

"You brought them there to lure me to your house," she said. "I'm not stupid, Luca." There was a long silence. "I'm almost at the marina," she said. "I will find you, and you better not have hurt one hair on either of their heads."

"Veda, wait for Enzo. He's on his way. Let him make sure you're safe." I walked over to the office door and opened it. "If not for my sake, then for your own. For your parents."

"Since when do you care about my safety? Really?" was all she said.

And then she hung up the phone.

"Fucking hell." I tossed Enzo's phone back to him. "Get to the marina. Cut her off before she can lead my fucking brother here. Make sure she wasn't followed. Get Veda and bring her here. I can't have her wandering around the area, trying to find me with my brother on her tail. Take the keys to the boat and bring her in that way. Send her friend home."

"Do you want me to go with him?" Tristan asked.

"No," I told him. "But take another vehicle and take care of anyone who might be tailing her without her knowledge. Make sure her friend is safe, then come back here. Enzo can handle Veda on his own."

The question was, could I?

CHAPTER 13
VEDA

"Dad! Mom!" I ran into Luca's house, not missing the fact that he wasn't there to greet me. Despite what I'd told him on the phone, my heart had raced the entire way there in anticipation of what he'd do when I walked in the door. But I ignored the pang in my chest caused by his absence. I wasn't here to see him. I was here to see my parents.

Running up the stairs, I made my way past his bedroom, holding my breath so I wouldn't catch even a whiff of his scent. I didn't think I'd be able to stand it. Once I was far enough down the hall, I sucked in air and paused at the last door where Enzo had told me my parents were being kept.

But when I got there, I wasn't prepared for the sight that greeted me, and I froze just inside the doorway.

My father sat in the chair next to the bed with his back to me, his shoulders hunched like he carried the weight of the world on his back. His elbows were on his knees and his head was in his hands, and I wondered if he'd dozed off. But then he lifted his head and looked over at the bed. I could see purplish swelling on the side of his face.

Reluctantly, I forced my eyes over to the bed where my mother lay still as a corpse. She was in the middle of the mattress, still wearing a hospital gown. It made her look as small as a child. An IV bag hung from a stand near the headboard, the line traveling to her right arm where the needle was taped in place inside her elbow. There was bruising around her wrist. Her other arm was in a full cast.

I could hear her labored breathing from where I stood, like she had to force herself to drag air into her lungs with each inhale. And on every exhale, she moaned softly, bitching even when she was unconscious. Her blonde hair was spread over the pillow and the blankets were pulled up, covering her from the waist down.

My feet moved without thought, taking me closer to the bed where my mother lay injured. As I got closer, I could see what had been done to her face.

"Oh my god." I slapped a hand over my mouth to prevent any more sounds from escaping, horrified at what I was seeing.

One side of my mother's gently beautiful face was all purple and red and yellow, her eye swollen shut from someone's fist hitting her repeatedly. The other side looked like it had been sliced open from her mouth to her ear. There had to be at least twenty or more stitches holding her face together.

"Veda! Oh, thank god!" I was grabbed from the side and pulled into my father's arms, even though he grunted in pain as he squeezed me tight. "Thank god you're okay."

"What the hell happened?" I asked him when I was able to pull away far enough to look at him. Much like my mother, his face was discolored and swollen. One hand went to his ribs, and I led him back to his chair so he could sit down again. "Are you okay?"

He waved his other hand in the air and made a face, dismissing my question as unimportant. "I'm fine, honey. A few broken ribs." His eyes were pulled to mom. "Your mother got the worst of it."

"Who did this?" I asked him.

Dad shook his head. "I don't know. They broke into the house when we were asleep. I tried to fight them off..." His voice broke, and I held my questions until he could get himself together. "There were three of them." He turned to me, his eyes beseeching, begging me to understand. "There was nothing I could do. Two of them had me down on the floor while the other one, the big one, went after your mom. There was nothing I could do..." His words trailed off as tears ran down his cheeks. "I tried, honey. I really tried. They had guns..."

Bending down to him, I grabbed him up in my arms much as he had to me just a minute ago. "Shhh...it's okay, Dad. This isn't your fault."

"No, it's yours," a raspy voice said.

I stiffened and helped Dad as he struggled to rise from his chair and sit on the side of the bed. He took my mother's hand in both of his. "Nancy? Do you need anything, sweetheart?" he asked her.

My mother's one good eye never left my face, her lips pressed together into a white line. When my father asked her again if she needed anything, she just shook her head slightly.

I'd never felt such hatred from her. It vibrated in the air between us, thick with tension.

Lifting my chin, I tried not to take it personally. She'd just been through a traumatic experience, and in true form, was looking for someone to blame. And, as always, that someone was me. "I'm so sorry this happened to you, Mom."

She clicked her tongue in disgust, and I could see the pain around her eyes just that small movement caused. "It happened because of you," she said, her voice gaining some clarity now, though she spoke while moving her lips as little as possible to avoid pulling on the stitches.

I shook my head. No. This wasn't because of me. This was because of Mario. Because of Luca. Not me. I didn't ask for any of this, and I tried to make her understand that. "What happened to you was beyond my control, Mom. I couldn't have stopped it."

Except...I could have, couldn't I? If I had just gotten Mario the information he wanted, if I'd just not gotten caught trying to find it, all of this could have been avoided. My parents would be safe and sound in their home, and perhaps I'd be the one lying in a hospital bed. Or worse. A sacrifice I would've happily made to keep them safe.

My thoughts must've shown on my face, because she narrowed her one good eye and nodded. "Because of you," she insisted.

"Sweetheart, this wasn't Veda's fault. She couldn't have known this would happen." My father, as always, tried to stick up for me.

"Whore!" she raged, her voice a sharp rasp. If she could've spit on me, I think she would have.

My father gave me an apologetic look as I backed up from the bed, a fist squeezing my heart until the pressure rose up into my throat, making it hard to speak. "I'm sorry you're upset with me," I choked out. "But I'm here to get you both out of here. We need to leave. Where are your things?" There was no way in hell I was leaving my parents here where I couldn't keep an eye on them. And I couldn't stay.

My father leaned down and murmured something to my mom, then gave her a kiss on the temple. "I'll be right back," he said as he let go of her hand.

I turned and proceeded him out the door and into the hallway, grateful to be out from under the weight of shame my mother wouldn't let me escape. He pulled it shut behind him. "She doesn't mean it," he told me as soon as we were alone.

A sarcastic laugh burst from me before I could stop it. "Yes, she does."

His expression was solemn. "Those men, Veda. They did...unimaginable things to her."

That's where he was wrong. I *could* imagine. Clearly. I wondered how my mother would feel if I showed her my own scar? It seemed to be Mario's calling card. I couldn't help but feel glad mine wasn't on my face.

"We both tried to fight," he went on. "Your mother"—an expression of pride flashed across his beaten face—"she was more than they bargained for. But in the end, there was nothing we could do." His shoulders began to shake with silent sobs, and I took his hand. I'd never understand what it was he saw in a woman like my mother, but he truly loved her. As did I. Just like I'd loved my sister. After all, she was still my blood.

"One of them pulled out a gun, and I had no choice but to watch as they...they...my god, Veda." His voice broke. "They raped her. Right in front of me. They beat her to a pulp, and they raped her. There was nothing I could do." He lost it then. Great, heaving sobs making him crumple where he stood.

I reached for him and, closing my eyes, I wrapped my arms around as much of him as I could, holding him upright. When I opened them, over his shoulder, I met icy blue eyes.

"They would've had to shoot me," Luca said in a deadly voice, "if it were us in that situation. It's the only way any of them would've laid a finger on you."

I held his gaze with tear-filled eyes as Dad, realizing someone else was here, straightened and wiped at his face. "That's because you're just as fucked up as they are," I told him.

"Veda," my father admonished. "This man was kind enough to bring us here, where we would be safe until we can figure out what to do."

"This man is the reason you're here, Dad. Not me. Don't let him shame you because you're not a cold-blooded killer."

Luca smiled, but there was no kindness there.

"And I'm taking my parents out of here," I told him. "Right now."

"And where are you going to go?"

"Anywhere but here," I said.

We stood at a standoff until my dad interrupted our staring contest. "Veda, I don't think we should move your mother. The ride here from the hospital was hard on her. She needs to rest. To heal."

"She can heal when we get somewhere else." I tried to make him understand. "It's not safe here, Dad, despite whatever bullshit he's been telling you." My eyes flicked to Luca, who still stood in the middle of the hall, watching us, watching *me*, and then back to my father. "Did he tell you it was his brother who did this to you? Did he tell you why?"

"We don't know that for sure," Luca hedged.

But he was lying. I stepped around my father to face him head on. "Are you being serious right now?" I asked. "Who the hell else would it have been?"

He didn't respond.

I grabbed my father's arm to take him back into the room to get their things. "Come on, Dad. We have to get out of here. Can mom walk?" I pointed at Luca. "And you're not going to stop us."

But Dad pulled away and threw up his hands. "Veda, honey, we can't go with you. I know it was the man who was engaged to your sister who did this to us. Well, not him, but his goons. They didn't admit it outright, but I know. What I don't know is why they did this, and honestly, right now, I don't care. All I care about is having somewhere safe for your mother and I to heal. And your friend here—"

"He's not my friend." I didn't know what he was, but a "friend" certainly wasn't it.

"And *Luca*," he emphasized his name, "took us in and offered us shelter." He paused, waiting for me to meet his eyes. "I'm not blind, Veda. I know what kind of man he is. And that's exactly why I think this is the safest place for us. And why you should stay here, too. With us."

I stared up at him in disbelief. "Dad, that man kept me prisoner here."

My father frowned. "That's not what you told us. You told us you were a guest here. To keep you safe."

"I lied. So you wouldn't worry. He's not witness protection, Dad."

"No," he said after a pause. "He's not. And that's why I know this is the safest place we can be."

I could tell by the stubborn tilt of his chin that I wasn't going to get my way with this. "I can't stay here," I whispered. "We can't stay here." Not because it wasn't safe for them. Because it wasn't safe for me. "Daddy, please come with me. We can go back to the hospital. We can tell the police everything and they can have guards there." Sammy was right. I should've gone to the cops as soon as I was able. I didn't even care that Luca could hear me.

"They did have guards there," my father informed me. "And Luca's men got into your mother's room anyway. Took us from right under their noses. I hate to think what would've happened if I hadn't been there and it wasn't Luca's men who came for us."

Son of a bitch.

Luca approached us, stopping only when I glared at him hard. "You should listen to your father," he told me. "Stay here where you're safe."

"Am I?" I asked him. "Safe?"

He didn't respond. But I hadn't really expected him to.

"Honey, I need to get back to your mother."

I wasn't going to win this battle. Not right now anyway. "Swear to me that my parents will come to no harm here with you."

"Why would I let any harm come to your parents?"

"Swear it, Luca."

"On my honor," he said without hesitation. "They will be safe here."

That would have to be enough. I couldn't get my parents out without help because my father was right; Mom was in no condition to be moved again. "Okay, Dad. Go ahead. I'll be back to check in on you guys again soon." I stared at Luca while I said this, daring him to deny me the right to come and go as I pleased.

But he just shoved his hands in his front pockets and watched us as I carefully hugged my dad and shut the bedroom door behind him. "Call me if you need anything," I told him. With one last warning look at Luca, I turned to leave.

"Veda."

"No." I kept walking. I couldn't talk to him right now.

"Veda, we need to talk."

"I have nothing to say to you." Jesus, I had to get out of here. Even just his voice had chills racing across my over-sensitized skin.

"Veda, you're not leaving here until you let me say what I have to say."

I spun around. "Okay, Luca. Fine. Let's talk. Where were *you?*"

His head cocked to the side, and his brows lowered in a frown. "I've been right here," he said carefully.

"No." I shook my head. "You said Mario's men would've had to kill you before you let them hurt me. So, where were *you* when I was the one being beaten and abused? Where were you when Mario woke me up by jizzing all over my face. Where were you when he held me down and...and..." I couldn't even finish the thought. "Where were you when *I* needed you to save me?" My voice clogged with tears before I could get it all out. I knew I was being irrational. But this shit that happened with my parents had my emotions riding the surface, raw and ugly. Emotions I'd thought I'd handled after Mario gave me back to Luca. Apparently, they'd just been suppressed.

He took a step toward me. Stopped. His bright blue eyes roamed over my face as he carefully chose his words. "I looked for you, *amore*. We looked everywhere. Did everything we could to find you."

That's what he'd told me. But suddenly, I was full of doubt. "Did you? Really?" How could I believe him after everything he'd done to me? I pointed my finger at the center of his chest. "And don't you dare fucking lie to me."

He caught my hand in his and used it to pull me closer to him. His other hand rose to hold my jaw between his fingers. His eyes searched mine and his scent—dark and clean—surrounded me, making me want to burrow into his arms. "I looked for you every fucking minute of every fucking day. I couldn't eat. I couldn't sleep." His brows lowered, and I could see the disbelief in his expression that I would even ask such a thing. "I went fucking insane, my *vita*, knowing he had you. Imagining what he was doing to you. Not knowing if you were alive or dead. My god, if he had hurt you—"

"He *did* hurt me."

His mouth snapped shut and his fingers tightened in my hair and on my face. "I got you back alive, *amore*. And your scars will heal over time."

"What if they don't?" I whispered.

"They will." He sounded so sure.

"Do you feel any remorse?" I asked him suddenly. I honestly wanted to know. "Any at all?"

There wasn't an ounce of hesitation with his answer. "For what my brother did to you and your parents, yes. Of course, I do. I'm not a heartless monster, Veda. No matter what you might think of me. But remorse for bringing you into my life?" His blue eyes darkened possessively. "No. I don't regret that. Not for one goddamned *fucking* second."

CHAPTER 14
LUCA

The moment I saw her step foot inside of my home, *her* home, I knew I would do it all again, and more, to have this woman. I'd give up everything. My business. My honor. My *life*. I couldn't escape the truth of that any longer. I would do whatever it took, kill whoever I had to, to keep her with me. My *vita*. Somehow, she'd crawled under my skin and burrowed her way into the deepest parts of me. She was mine.

And I was hers.

More tears filled her eyes until they shone like a stormy sea. "Why are you doing this to me?" she asked.

"I'm only giving you the truth you asked for, *amore*."

"It's too late for your truth," she sneered at me. "You've ruined me, Luca. Destroyed my life. My family. You used me. Forced me to share your bed..."

"And you fucking liked it."

She stiffened, and then she came at me with wild eyes, her small fists swinging at my face. And because a sick part of me enjoyed this side of her, I let her get in a few good hits before I grabbed her wrists and forced them behind her back, then hauled her against my body so she could feel how much I'd missed her as I dragged her down the hall, away from her parents' room. "How is this my fault, *amore*? I did not rape your mother. Nor did I beat your father to a bloody pulp. And you stayed in my bed willingly enough once I made you come."

"None of this would've happened if it wasn't for you," she seethed. "You're the one who brought me here! You and your petty games of revenge! My sister is dead! Why couldn't you have just left her that way? Why!" She struggled against me, trying to work her wrists loose from my grip. "Instead, you had to bring her back through me. Flaunt me in front of your brother. And now he's lost what was left of his mind. He went after my parents, Luca! My fucking parents!"

The only thing she managed to accomplish by fighting me was to envelop me in her scent and make my cock fucking hard. "If it wasn't for me, you never would've known what happened to her. She'd be lying in an unmarked grave in Mexico with no one to mourn her."

"I wish I'd never met you!" she gritted out. "You're a selfish son of a bitch. And I hate you!"

I narrowed my eyes. "You hate me?"

"Yes!"

A smile teased the corners of my mouth. "Should I take you to my room and show you how much of a liar you are, *amore?*"

She struggled some more. "Let me go, you bastard." Pulling back as far as she could, she spit in my face.

We both went utterly still. A deadly calm came over me as her eyes went wide with fear. I heard a clock tick somewhere down the hall. The front door opened and closed downstairs.

Her voice was hushed. "Luca...I didn't mean..."

"Oh, I think you did," I said quietly.

She shook her head, her blonde hair falling over her face and brushing the tops of her breasts. "No. No, I didn't. I just..."

I wiped my cheek on the shoulder of my jacket. Then I released her hands, bent down, and lifted her into my arms.

"Luca, where are you taking me?" she asked as I strode toward my room. She'd stopped struggling. She knew she'd taken things too far.

"To your punishment." Holding her close against my chest, I entered my room and kicked the door closed behind me before I set her on her feet. Then I turned the lock.

Her eyes shot around the room. "Luca, please. I'm sorry."

"Sorry for what, exactly? For not appreciating my help? For hitting me? Or for spitting in my face?"

She stilled, and I watched as the blood drained from her face. She was remembering what happened the last time she'd dared to raise a hand to me. "Luca, don't do this."

"I'm not going to do anything you don't deserve, *amore*."

She swallowed hard as I took off my jacket and tossed it onto the chair beside the bed. But when my fingers went to the buttons on my shirt, her gray eyes darkened. Her lips parted, and the tip of her tongue shot out to wet her bottom lip. She was not unaffected by me. And it had been way too long since she was naked beneath me.

She stared at my bare chest for a few seconds, then tore her eyes away. "I'm not fucking you."

"No," I told her. "You're not."

She stood, undecided, as she tried to figure out what I meant. Then, just as I finished unbuttoning the last button on my shirt, she shot to the right and tried to run out the door. But the lock held her up long enough for me to grab her and carry her with me to the bed.

"I'll scream!" she cried.

"Go ahead," I told her. "I'm sure your father will come running to your rescue. So if you want him to hear you moaning my name as he stands outside the locked door, you go ahead and scream." I sat down on the edge of the bed and dragged her facedown across my lap. She was wearing black, stretchy pants.

Perfect.

With one hand on the back of her neck to hold her down, I used the other to pull them down off her ass. She wasn't wearing any panties, and I growled my appreciation.

When she realized what I was doing, she went very still. But she didn't fool me. I knew it was only the calm before the storm, and I held my hand hovered over one smooth cheek.

As soon as she started to buck, I brought it down hard, my breaths coming hard as her fair skin blushed pink beneath my palm.

"Goddammit, Luca! Don't you dare! I'm not a child!"

My hand came down again on the other side.

"Fuck you!" she spit out, kicking out with her legs and trying to push herself away from the bed.

Removing my hand from the back of her neck, I leaned down and caught her wrists, stretching them above her head across the bed as my leg came down over hers, trapping her on my lap. Unable to move, she shrieked with frustration.

"Do I need to gag you, too?" I asked her as I rubbed my palm over the heated skin of her ass. "It wouldn't be ideal, because then I'll miss the lusty moans that'll soon be leaving those pretty lips. But I'll do it if I have to. I really don't want to knock out your father just so I can deal out your punishment."

She sank her teeth into my thigh.

I cursed, and my hand smacked her ass hard enough to make her let go. "Do that again," I dared her.

"Fuck you."

"Is that the only thing you have to say to me?" I spanked her again, and again, as I told her how incredibly insane she made me. Told her how much I wanted her. The things I wanted to do to her. I laid my palm to her ass until she was no longer cursing at me but squirming on my lap, and those low moans I loved to hear were escaping her lips no matter how much she tried to stop them.

Dipping two fingers between her fleshy thighs, I slid them into the folds of her cunt. She was so fucking wet, my own moan couldn't be contained as my cock kicked up against her stomach. "This," I told her. "This is mine." I was so hard I felt like I was about to burst from my skin.

I leaned over her, pressing my lips to her hair. "You're so fucking wet for me."

"Not for you," she panted.

"You're angry," I told her. "And you're scared. But don't ever lie to me, Veda." I inserted one finger inside of her, then two, fire heating my blood when the muscled walls tightened around them.

"I'm not fucking you," she told me again.

I smiled, and pressed my thumb into the puckered hole of her ass. "This is mine, too."

"No." But even as she tried to deny me, she rolled her hips so I would go deeper. I didn't give her what she wanted, though. Not yet.

I pulled out my fingers, spreading her moisture through her cunt and up to her ass. "Have you fucked anyone else after you ran from me?"

"Luca, stop," she pleaded.

"Have you?"

"None of your fucking business," she spit out.

I tightened my grip around her wrists. "If you have"—I rimmed her ass with my thumb—"I'll find out. And I will kill him. But it's up to you if his death is quick and easy or long and painful. So, tell me"—I cupped her in my hand, pressing the tip of my thumb inside her tight ass and finding her clit with my fingers—"have you let anyone else touch you like this?"

"Please," she begged, pushing her hips back into my hand.

I stopped moving my hand. "Tell. Me."

"No!" she burst out. "No! Of course not. I've been too busy trying to stay alive, you ass."

With a growl of possession, I sank my thumb all the way in as my fingers rubbed her clit. Veda cried out, burying her face in the comforter, and I felt her muscles contract as she came.

I used her pleasure and my thumb to relax the ring of muscles, preparing her for what was to come. There were no thoughts in my head, just this obsessive need to be inside of her everywhere.

Releasing her wrists, I smoothed her hair and ran my hand down her back to the bottom of her shirt, lifting it to expose the smooth skin of her back. There were no scars here. Nothing to mar the perfection other than a few freckles.

Slowly, I removed my thumb, her body gripping me tight to try to hold me there. When it was out, I shoved her pants down her legs, slipping off her shoes.

"I'm not fucking you," she repeated. But her voice lacked the conviction of earlier and her fists gripped the comforter above her head.

"No, you're not. I'm fucking you," I told her. "Everywhere."

Before she could argue with me, I ran my hand up the back of one leg and then another. I couldn't get enough of the feel of her skin. I rubbed both hands over her back and legs, kneading her sore ass as she lay sprawled across my lap.

I had to have her. All of her. Nothing else mattered to me right now. The entire fucking house could burn down around me, and I don't think I'd even notice. Veda was here. And she was everything. And she was MINE.

Lifting her off my lap as I stood, I sat her on the bed and removed her shirt, then my own. "Don't fucking move." My eyes never left her as I kicked off my shoes and took off my slacks, socks, and boxer briefs until I was as naked as she was. The fading "M" carved into her chest made violence rise inside of me, taunting me with the reminder that Mario had laid his hands on her. Had his dick in her sweet mouth. And I wondered if I would always have this rush of frantic need to possess her every time I saw it.

I cupped her cheek in my hand and lifted her face to mine. My *vita* stared up at me with rebellious eyes even as her luscious lips parted for my kiss and her soft, plump breasts rose and lowered with each panting breath. I had things I wanted to say. So many fucking things. The words were there on the tip of my tongue, all running together until finally I ducked my head and took her mouth with mine.

With that kiss, I told her all of the things I was feeling. The awe. The anger. The raw, dangerous wanting I had for her.

The need to possess her utterly until there was no one in her life or her body but me.

I continued to kiss her as I pressed her back on the mattress and covered her body with mine. She was soft where I was hard. Warm where I was cold. Light where I was dark. She was everything. She was perfect.

And she was mine.

Hesitantly, her arms came up to wrap around my neck, and I deepened the kiss. I couldn't get enough of her. She tasted like summer fruit, sweet and fleeting. And I was afraid if I stopped, she would disappear from my life again.

The feel of her hands on my back, shoulders, and arms was both overwhelming and not enough. I needed more of her touch. More of everything. And I fucking needed it now.

With a nip of her bottom lip, I moved down her body, tasting the raised skin of her scars before taking one hard nipple into my mouth and then the other. Her nails dug into my skin as she moaned, her legs falling open to accommodate me between them as she arched her back, offering me her body.

But it wasn't enough. I wanted all of her. Every breath. Every beat of her heart. Every thought and every fear. I wanted her soul.

She no longer fought me as I made my way down to the sweetest part of her. I inhaled the musky scent of her desire, and my mouth watered with the anticipation of tasting her. But I held myself back, teasing her with wet kisses on her belly and thighs until she dug her fingers into my skull and forcibly brought my mouth to her cunt, rubbing her soft flesh on my lips with wanton abandon as little cries of frustration escaped her lips.

Only then did I give her what she wanted, holding her hips down on the bed with one arm thrown across her lower stomach and running my tongue from her ass to her clit. As I worked her with my tongue, I pressed two fingers against the entrance to her ass. She tensed when she first felt me, relaxing only when I distracted her with my mouth. Then, and only then, did I press them into the tight passage, stretching her more.

Veda cried out my name, her heels digging into the mattress to escape even as her orgasm slammed into her. I kept going as she shuddered around me, sliding my fingers in and out of her ass as my tongue milked every drop from her body.

She was still riding it out when I rose over her and flipped her onto her stomach. I didn't want to see my brother's mark on her. Not now.

Lining up the head of my cock with her cunt, I pushed my way in, stopping partway inside of her to lift her hips until she was on her knees with her gorgeous ass in the air, the skin still pink and heated from my hand. With one hand on her hip and one on the center of her back to hold her down, I started pumping in and out, slamming into her so hard I felt her womb. She widened her legs, opening herself more to me, and I slapped her ass, then kneaded the heated flesh before wetting my thumb in my mouth.

This fuckable part of her was as perfect as the rest. Pink and tight. And mine. All fucking mine.

My balls tightened, and I slowed down, pressing my thumb inside of her as far as it would go.

She stiffened beneath me. "Luca...no..."

Then one finger, then two...

"This is mine," I told her. "All of you, Veda. I need all of you."

CHAPTER 15
VEDA

The pressure in my ass was soothed only when he pulled out of my pussy and put his mouth on me, spreading my cheeks with his hands. I tried to tell him no. I knew this would hurt. But he wouldn't listen.

I panicked and tried to crawl away, but Luca grabbed my hips and held me there as he lubed me up with his tongue.

I didn't know what to do. Despite what I told him, I needed this insanity that always happened between us. And I wanted him inside of me again. Desperately. But I'd never been fucked in the ass before. And I was scared.

But god, what he was doing felt so good.

Reaching beneath me, his hand covered my breast, kneading it in his palm as his amazing mouth lingered on my core, licking my ass, my clit, and everywhere in between.

By the time he rose up behind me, I was a quivering mess. I loved the way he needed control. I craved the way he took me whenever he wanted me, like his need to have me was too much for him to contain. How he didn't give me a choice. And honestly, I didn't fucking want one. No one ever turned me on the way Luca did.

I loved the way he loved me.

His hands spread the cheeks of my ass and I knew he was looking at me. I wasn't embarrassed. He made me feel beautiful. Precious. Like I was the only woman in the world for him. I pushed my hips back, craving his cock, and he groaned. I felt his thumb dip into the folds of my pussy and then spread the moisture around the rim of my ass.

"You are mine, Veda. My *vita*." His voice was gruff and breathless.

"Yes," I admitted, so quietly I didn't think he heard.

"Yes," he answered.

There was pressure, more than before, and I stiffened.

Luca moaned, and the pressure eased. But only for a moment before he was back, the wide head of his cock forcing its way inside my ass. "Let me in," he ordered.

My only answer was to whimper softly as the pressure became almost unbearable.

"Breathe, *amore*."

I tried. I really did.

"God, you're so fucking tight."

More pressure, and then it eased as he pulled out. I moaned at the feeling his withdrawal produced. Fuck, I never knew it could feel like this. I tried to relax as he tried again. It was getting a little easier now. Still painful, but not as bad.

"Touch yourself," he told me.

I slid one arm beneath my body until my fingers were on my clit. My pussy was so wet. Gently, I rubbed my clit as he pressed inside of me. "Oh my god." Holy fuck. Almost immediately, my lower belly clenched tight with pleasure, then released, only to do it again, stronger this time. "Luca." His name was a moan on my lips every time he pulled out, only to push inside of me again.

"Yes, *amore*." His hands tightened on my hips. "Tight. So fucking tight. Ah," I closed my eyes and tried to breathe, "I'm gonna come before I even get inside of you."

Pleasure and pain rolled through me with each slow surge of his hips and every flick of my fingers. My womb tightened and released with wave upon wave of my oncoming orgasm and nothing coherent came out of my mouth, just little whimpering noises I couldn't stop.

Luca pulled out again, and my hips tried to follow. I felt his fingers on my ass as he lubed me up with my own wetness, and then he was back, the head of his cock slipping inside of me. His fingers tightened on my hips. He pulled back a bit, and then with one great push, he was there.

His growl of possession mingled with my cry as my orgasm rose within me, the waves of pleasure coming faster and faster.

"Not yet," he gritted out. "Wait for me, *amore*."

I stilled my fingers as he began to work his way even deeper inside of me, thrusting in and out until I felt his hips touch my ass. "Now," he told me. "Now, Veda." His breathing was harsh and erratic. "Fuck. I'm gonna come in your ass."

My fingers found my clit again, and I worked myself as he took my ass, with a few slow strokes at first, and then quickly thrusting harder and faster. "Mine," he growled. "Fucking all of you."

His name tore from my lips as the most intense orgasm I'd ever had crashed over me, and my body jerked uncontrollably as I turned my face into the mattress to smother my cries. Luca's weight came down on top of me and with a deep cry, his cock deep in my ass, he came inside of me so hard I felt every pulse of his cock.

My legs couldn't hold me anymore and I collapsed onto my stomach. He followed me down, still inside of me, holding most of his weight off of me with his arms. Luca buried his face into the side of my neck. "Mine," he growled, dropping kisses on the sensitive spot between my neck and shoulder. "Every fucking part of you."

I would've argued with him, but I didn't have the energy. Besides, who was I kidding? He was absolutely right.

"Thank you," he breathed in my ear. "For trusting me not to hurt you. I would never hurt you, Veda."

"You were going to shoot me in the head in front of your brother." There was no accusation in my voice. It was said as a fact. I didn't even mention the fascination he seemed to have with his knife.

He sighed heavily. "We've been over this, *amore*."

"You almost choked me out in the gym." My mouth kept running, no matter how much I tried to stop. "You threatened me with a knife...more than once." Okay, so I did mention it.

He stilled, and his voice was coldly violent when he said, "I am not the one who used that knife to mark you." Carefully, he pulled out of me and rolled off to the side. I stayed as I was and turned my head to face him.

He brushed my hair out of my face. "You are my life. My *vita*. To hurt you would only be to destroy myself."

I studied the hard man beside me. I wanted to believe him. I truly did. "What will you do for me, Luca?"

"Anything, *amore*. I would do anything."

"Will you let me walk out of here again?"

He stared at me for a long moment. "Yes. As long as I come with you."

I closed my eyes. I never should've come back. "I don't want you to come with me. I want to go home."

"This is your home."

But I shook my head. "No. It's not. It can't be."

His bright blue eyes traveled over my face, studying me, searching for the lie in my words. But I kept it hidden deep down inside of me so he wouldn't find it. I couldn't give in to him. Not this time. If I did, I'd never come back from it. My fate would be tied with his forever. Luca throwing me out to the wolves when he caught me in his office was the most heartbreaking thing I'd ever gone through, even more so than when he was going to shoot me in front of Mario, and it had taught me something new about the rules of this world. To come back here had been stupid and reckless of me.

He was still moving the pieces on the board. Bringing my parents here had been nothing but a strategic move on his part to get me back into his home, and in my haste to make sure they were all right, I'd played right into his hands.

Luca sat up suddenly, and I couldn't help but run my eyes over his strong shoulders and back, honed by all of the hours he spends in his gym. Against my will, I felt the stirrings of renewed desire. "I want you here. With me." His voice had a tone of finality in it.

Pulling the comforter up around me, I rolled over and gingerly sat up with my back against the headboard. I was suddenly so tired. "I want to go back to my friend's apartment until such time my parents are able to be moved. And then I plan to take them and disappear."

His head whipped toward me, and I was caught in the iciness of his eyes. "No."

I shivered, but not from the cold, and pulled the comforter up closer around me. "Luca, this world you inhabit isn't for me. I don't belong here."

His eyes narrowed, and I could see that he didn't miss something very important that I hadn't said. I never said I didn't want to be with *him*.

Without a word, he rose from the bed and walked naked across the room to the bathroom. A few seconds later, I heard the shower come on.

I stared at the open door as I took stock of my body. I felt thoroughly fucked, and only a little bit sore. Less so than I thought I would. After a moment, I got up and followed him.

His eyes shot to me when I joined him in the shower, and I caught a flash of surprise right before they wandered over my body with just as much intensity as the first time he saw me like this, and his arms slowly fell back to his sides. "My father held a meeting tonight with the more powerful members of the family to discuss who would replace him when he steps down."

I stepped under the spray, schooling my features to hide my shock. He'd never volunteered information like this to me before. Usually, he told me what I absolutely needed to know and no more. I started to wet my hair as I waited for him to continue.

He picked up the shampoo and poured some into his hand, then stepped behind me and began to massage it into my scalp. "The other details aren't important, but there's one you should know."

I closed my eyes as I allowed him to take care of me. It felt good, and it seemed to distract him from the fact that he was sharing with me.

"Luigi, my father, laid down the law to the entire family. Mario is not to be harmed. He will take over my father's position when the time comes."

"What does that mean?"

"It means my brother will be in a position of complete power."

"And what if someone disobeys that decision?"

He tilted my head back under the spray to rinse the shampoo from the long strands. "The repercussions would be fatal. He will consider it a direct insult to his honor if anyone disobeys his order."

"What about your honor?" I asked him. "Your life? My life?"

His hand fell away from me, and I wiped the water from my face to look at him. A muscle ticked in his jaw and his nostrils flared with the effort to keep himself under control. "He doesn't give a fuck about my honor. As a matter of fact, he doesn't give a fuck about me at all."

"But you're his son, too. How can he do that to you?"

He looked at me then. "How does your mother do it to you?" Lifting his hand, he rubbed the back of his knuckles down my cheek. "I should consider myself lucky he hasn't cut me out of the family completely." Then he took a breath and picked up the shower pouf and body wash. Lathering it up, he began to wash me, holding me steady with his other hand. The more he touched me, the more I could see the tension leave his jaw and shoulders. "Stay with me tonight."

Immediately, I shook my head. "I can't."

"What if I don't give you a choice?"

"Is that what you're doing?"

There was no hesitation in his answer. "Yes."

I sighed, but I didn't fight with him. What was the use? It wouldn't get me anywhere. And honestly, although I would never admit it, I'd missed him, too.

He squatted down to wash my legs and feet, dropping a kiss on my inner thigh. "This world you spoke of...my world."

"Mmm..."

"It's all that I know. And you, Veda, are a part of it now." He rose to his full height and began to wash himself as I rinsed off, his eyes never leaving me.

"What if I don't want to be a part of it."

"That's not possible now."

"And I have to stay with you because you're the only one who can keep me safe from Mario. Right?"

He gave me a nod. "I will never let anything happen to you, *amore*."

I smiled at him, but it was a sad smile, because I knew he was wrong. There was nothing he'd be able to do. Hell, even I knew that. He was just in denial. "Luca, if Mario takes over your father's position, what do you think he will do? He's not going to let us live in peace. He'll come for you. And for me. And you won't be able to stop him, will you?"

"That won't happen."

"But..."

"Veda, stop." Taking me into his arms, I felt his erection press into my stomach. "It won't happen. I won't let it. But you need to give me time to figure things out since my father—and the way I feel for you—put a glitch in my original plan. Will you do that for me?" He brushed my lips with his, then dropped kisses along my jaw, my throat...

"Okay," I whispered as I wrapped my arms around his wet shoulders. "But I'm not your prisoner anymore, Luca."

"No, *amore*. You are my life. Something I cherish much more."

CHAPTER 16
LUCA

I woke up the next morning with Veda sprawled across my chest and her hair tickling my nose. Even in sleep, I held her tight against me, my arms wrapped around her in a vice-like hold and one leg thrown over hers. Glancing over at my phone on the nightstand, I was surprised at the time. For the first time in weeks, I'd slept completely through the night.

She sighed when I loosened my hold and rubbed my palms against the soft skin of her back, but didn't wake. So I gently moved her off of me and pulled the blankets up around her waist before I got out of bed. She laid on her stomach with her arms bent out from her body, her hands shoved under the pillows and her face turned toward me. Her lips were parted in sleep, and her soft wheat-blonde hair was spread across her bare shoulders and her pillow. I stared down at her for a moment, then I picked up my phone and took a picture. I wanted to hold this image of her forever.

Veda was still asleep when I came out from my shower and got dressed. I pressed my lips to her temple and cheek, but she didn't stir. So I grabbed my jacket off the chair and then gently closed the bedroom door behind me and made my way downstairs to get some coffee and check in with Enzo and Tristan.

Three hours later, we were about to head out to do rounds at the clubs when I got a phone call. I frowned when I saw the name on the screen. "Rene? What's going on?" I wasn't expecting to hear from Maria's brother for a while. Not until he'd taken care of a little "problem" happening on his end of things that was putting a glitch in our usual shipment. "Did things get taken care of?"

"No, *amigo*. I wouldn't say that. As a matter of fact, my little issue has grown significantly larger and I'm not going to be able to get our usual shipment to you for a month. Maybe more."

"That's not going to work for me, Rene."

"*Si*, I am aware. And that's why I contacted one of my cousins to see if he could cover things for me this time around."

"And what did he say?"

"He said he would. But he would feel better if you were there personally to receive it from him. He's not familiar with your men, but he remembers you from Maria's funeral."

An unusual request, but not completely surprising, all things considered. Still... "I don't think I'll be able to make it. I have my own personal issues going on here. I can send Enzo or Tristan—"

"No. He wants you or no deal," Rene said. "Honestly, between you and me, my cousin is a little *loco*, and it makes him a little too suspicious sometimes. But as long as he knows you, he's cool. He'll make sure the job goes off without a hitch as long as you're the one who's there with the money."

Fucking hell. "It's really not a good time for me, my friend."

"Well, you better make it a good time, or this deal will have to be postponed."

That was not an option. Not with my father already up my ass, just waiting for a reason to call me out. I cursed softly and sighed. "When and where?"

"Can you be at the drop spot by tonight? The usual time."

"I can be there."

"Good. I'll tell him you're coming. His name is Jesus, and he looks like me. A few inches taller and a few pounds lighter."

"Easy enough."

"Call me if there are any issues at all. I'll have this shit straightened out on my end by next month, Luca. I promise you."

"I'll see you then." Hanging up the phone, I relayed the information to Enzo and Tristan.

"What of your guests?" Enzo asked. "Do you want me to stay here?"

I shook my head. "No. Even though Rene vouches for this guy, I don't know him. I want you both with me, just in case. We'll leave only the necessary amount of men to watch the house. It will only be for one night."

"And you're going to trust that Veda and her parents will still be here when we get back?"

I looked at Tristan. "No, I'm not. She's way too intelligent to leave alone. I'll leave Tony here to make sure they stay in the house."

"Tony?" Tristan asked. "I don't know if that's a good idea."

Enzo and I exchanged looks. "It would be one way to find out what he's up to," he said.

"Agreed. Perhaps I'm being too suspicious, but he's been acting strange lately. I would like to know for sure where his loyalties lie. Especially with Veda back in the house. We can keep an eye on him with the security cameras while we're driving. He'll be relaxed with just Vita and Lisa in the house. And if he says or does anything suspicious, I'll confront him when we get back."

"Do you trust him enough to leave him here alone?"

"No," I told Enzo. "Have two of the men outside on alert. If anything happens, they can hold Tony until we get back."

"I'll go let Tony know," Tristan said. "And the others."

I gave him a nod. "Don't let him see you. Be discreet. We'll need to leave in an hour. I'd like to get there early. Scope out the area before they arrive. Just in case this is a setup. Some way to get me out into the open." He gave me a nod and went to go find Tony.

Enzo took off his sunglasses and rubbed his eyes with his thumb and forefinger. "You think Mario would've gotten to Rene?"

The idea seemed ludicrous, even to me. Rene and I were almost like family. And if this was a trap, I knew without a shadow of a doubt Rene had been forced into it. But I wouldn't put anything past my brother. "It wouldn't surprise me. Despite our father's order, he must be feeling threatened right now. And as we know, my brother doesn't react well to being threatened."

"What's going on?"

We both turned to find Veda standing in the doorway. My eyes raked over her unconsciously, taking in every detail: her hair pulled back into a ponytail that fell over one shoulder, the too-big black T-shirt that was obviously mine, and the pair of loose, creamy shorts she must've found in our closet, left here from before. Her feet were bare. Toes painted a light peachy color that matched her nails.

Raising my eyes back to her face, I found the same hunger in hers that now burned deep within me. "How are your parents?" I asked her.

She quietly cleared her throat. "Pretty much the same as yesterday. My mother is crankier than usual, which is to be expected. Lisa's making her some soup that she'll be able to slurp up through a straw, although I don't know if that'll help. Dad won't leave her side, but I did coerce him into taking a shower just now. I gave him a pair of your sweatpants and a shirt to borrow." She frowned, as if just realizing something. "I hope that was alright."

"Of course," I assured her. "We can get them more of their things tomorrow after I make sure it's safe to go to their house."

"Thank you." She looked back and forth between us. "So, what's going on?"

"I'm going to go get things ready," Enzo said.

Veda smiled at him and moved out of the way so he could walk past. "Ready for what?"

"I have to go out of town," I told her, watching her expression closely. "Just for tonight. There's something I need to take care of, and Tristan and Enzo are coming with me."

A flash of disappointment crossed her face. "Oh." She opened her mouth. Closed it. Then blurted out, "Can't someone else do it?"

"No, *amore*. Not this time."

Crossing her arms, she stared down at her toes.

I closed the distance between us and cupped her jaw, tilting her chin up until her eyes met mine. "You'll be alright here. I'm going to leave men outside, and Tony will be here in the house with you and Lisa. You met him that day in my office."

"The day you were shot."

"Yes. And there'll be guards outside the house as well." I brushed my thumb over the lines of worry between her brows. "It's only for one night. I'll be back before you wake up tomorrow."

"What if something goes wrong?"

"It won't," I said with more conviction than I felt. I pressed my forehead to hers for a few seconds. "Please don't do anything stupid while I'm gone. And when I get back, you and I will talk." I kissed her head, then her sweet lips.

She was suspiciously quiet as we walked back out to the kitchen together, where I told Lisa what was going on. She agreed that she and her husband, Kevin, would be there in the house that night with Veda and her family.

I gave Veda one last kiss, running my fingers through the soft strands of her hair before laying it back down over the curve of her breast. "I'll see you tomorrow."

"Be careful," she told me.

I left her in the kitchen with Lisa and went to join my men.

CHAPTER 17
VEDA

*L*uca was only gone a few minutes when Tony found me in the kitchen, sitting at the table, drinking a cup of tea. Lisa was telling me her secret to making a great soup.

Wine.

"Hey, Lisa. Veda. I'm Tony."

He held his hand out, and I stood up to greet him. He was younger than Luca, but not by much, with dark hair and eyes and a clean-shaven face. Handsome, I guess. "Hi, Tony," I said, taking his hand. "We've met before."

He smiled, and like that day in Luca's office, there was way more interest there than there should've been as his eyes roved over my face and breasts. I'd barely noticed it then, distracted as I was by the fact Luca had been shot. Not until Luca said something to him. But I sure as hell noticed it now. "I wasn't sure if you'd remember me. But I guess you do." He winked at me as he let go of my hand, his fingers lingering on mine just a little longer than they should have, then walked over to the counter and poured himself a cup of coffee from the pot Lisa always kept fresh.

An idea began to form, and I disregarded it almost immediately, shoving it away as nothing short of crazy. But it kept creeping back in, churning around in my thoughts.

This guy obviously wasn't as scared of Luca as he should have been. Even Enzo didn't talk to me with such familiarity, or touch me in any way, shape, or form that could be seen as too intimate. Not even when we were training, just the two of us. It was all business with him then. And he certainly didn't ogle my tits. Ever.

But maybe that could work to my advantage. If this guy, Tony, was too busy thinking about me naked, maybe he wouldn't pay as much attention as he should be to what I was doing.

Of course, I might be totally misreading things. Maybe he was just a friendly guy, one who liked to flirt but never carried through with the promises in his eyes. And there was a good chance my plan wouldn't work at all. But my body was the only weapon I had at my disposal right now, and this was the only chance I was going to have to get myself and my parents out of here. Luca would be gone for less than twenty-four hours. That didn't give me much time to carry out the plan that was swiftly coming together in my head.

But maybe it would be enough time to set it in motion.

Luca thought he had me exactly where he wanted me—in his bed. And if I were honest with myself, I couldn't say that I didn't like being there. But what kind of life would I have with a man like him? This man who claimed I was his whole world was also the same man who had planned to take me out of it. The man who threw me out of this house, convinced I had betrayed him no matter how many times I told him I'd only done it to protect him—to protect us—from his psycho brother. But he hadn't cared. He'd given me back my freedom, but it was a freedom that could've very well cost me my life.

I'd rolled the dice twice with him. I don't think I'd be so lucky a third time.

No matter how much my heart longed for him, how much my body craved him, if I stayed, I would spend our life together tiptoeing around this beautiful house, scared to death I would unknowingly break some rule or insult his honor. And how many chances would he give me before my luck ran out?

It all came down to one thing. No matter what he told me, when it came to my life, I could trust him to keep me safe from anyone who would hurt me...except for him.

And I was the only one who could protect myself from him.

But the weird thing was, I didn't completely blame Luca for this. He was controlling. Obsessive. Violent. Possessive. I knew this. But he hadn't gotten that way on his own. It was the hostility between him and Mario that made him that way. A game of life and death with rules that were made up by their father, rules that changed mid-game, if I went by what Luca had told me last night. And the only way to win this battle between brothers was if one of them was in the ground.

I wasn't sticking around to see which one it was going to be. Because no matter who came out the winner, I had no doubt in my mind I would be the prize. And there was only a fifty-fifty chance it would be Luca who won me.

My mind made up, I excused myself to go check on my mother.

A few hours later, at dinner, I began to put my plan into action. After taking food up to my parents, Lisa left my dinner warming in the oven and had gone to eat with her husband, leaving me alone in the kitchen. I'd just taken it out when Luca's guard dog stuck his head in to check on me, right on time.

"You doing okay, Veda?"

"Hey, Tony," I said with a smile. But not too much of a smile. I didn't want to expose my hand too soon. "Why don't you stay? Keep me company while I eat?"

His eyes wandered down my body and back to my face, slower on the way up. I'd changed into a pair of tight jean shorts and a red, fitted, cotton shirt with a neckline that scooped low in the back and was held together with criss-cross laces, exposing plenty of skin. "I don't know if that's such a good idea."

"Are you sure? There's lots of food here. Lisa made meatloaf and potatoes." I gave him a sad smile. "It's my dad's favorite, but he won't leave my mom to come eat with me, so she took his plate upstairs. I'd go eat up there, but I'm not exactly my mom's favorite person right now." I rolled my eyes. "Annnd that's a story for another time."

He stood in the doorway, undecided.

"Come on," I told him. "Grab a plate and help yourself."

He waited until I was done serving myself before coming in to get himself a plate. I sat at the small kitchen table instead of going into the dining room, leaving him with the choice of having a cozy dinner with me or taking his plate to the counter and eating there.

He chose to come sit by me.

I popped open a bottle of wine and poured myself a glass, but I didn't offer him any. "I assume you're on the job," I offered as an explanation.

"You would be right," he told me. "But a glass or two won't hurt." He took a bite of his dinner as I got up to get another glass for him. "This is damn good meatloaf."

"Lisa's a great cook."

We ate in silence for a few minutes, and then he said, "So, tell me about this beef your mother has with you."

A trickle of unease crept down my spine. Yet, I wasn't exactly sure why. It was an innocent enough question, considering what I'd told him a minute ago. "Oh, that's a long story that started with my birth."

"That bad, huh?"

"Pretty much."

He looked around the kitchen, empty except for the two of us. "I think we've got time."

Taking a drink of my wine, I figured, what the hell. "Well, for one, I was born with what my mother considers a birth defect. Unlike my sister, who was perfect in every way since birth. I don't even think she cried as a baby."

"What was wrong with you?"

"A heart thing that was easily fixed with surgery."

"You were a twin, right? And your sister was engaged to Luca's brother, Mario?"

Again, I had that uneasy feeling. I mean, as one of Luca's guys, I assumed the story of how I'd gotten here was common knowledge by now. However, if I remembered right, Luca told Tony who I was the first time we met. So, why the question now? I decided to play along. "Um, yeah."

He nodded and shoved a forkful of potatoes into his mouth. "So, go on. You were born defective..."

I laughed, and that uneasy feeling gradually went away. Over the next hour, I told him what it was like growing up with my mother and sister. I also polished off four glasses of wine.

"So, basically, you've been told what to do your entire life by first your mother and then your sister."

"Yup. Sounds about right."

He put his elbows on the table and leaned forward. He was uncomfortably close, and the little hairs rose on my arms. "And they both under-appreciated you, and still do, for the beautiful, capable woman you've become."

I pressed my back into my chair. "My father seems to think so, at least."

"I think your papa is right. I think maybe the people in your life don't know the treasure they have in you."

I turned my glass around on the table, unsure of how to respond. Did he mean my family? Or Luca? *Don't chicken out now, Veda. This is exactly what you wanted.* "That's sweet of you to say."

He reached across the small space between us and covered my hand with his. "I mean every word, Veda. You deserve better than a man like Luca."

Wow. That was easy. "Are you telling me that you're that man?"

His fingers played with mine. I knew I should pull away, should play hard to get, but my head felt muddled, and my blood was warmed by the wine. "I could be," he told me. "If you'd let me."

I pulled my hand away from his. "Not while I'm in this house. Luca would kill you."

"Luca gets a little too full of himself sometimes. And I could get you out of here. Put you up somewhere safe."

I almost laughed aloud. This was playing out just like an old mafia movie. "Are you offering to make me your mistress? Do people still do that?"

He smiled at my question, but there was little humor in it. His eyes flashed. A warning. "I'm offering you a way to be free."

"By leaving this prison for a different one?" *Shut your damn mouth, Veda. This is what you wanted.* But I couldn't help it. What the hell was it with these Italian guys thinking us poor, weak females couldn't survive on our own? Were they all like this? Or just this particular group? All I needed was a little help getting past the guards out front, not a sugar daddy for life.

But he wasn't deterred just yet. "Ah, but it wouldn't be a prison, *bella.* You're much too beautiful to keep locked in a tower." His eyes roamed over my face. "No. You'd be free to do whatever you wanted. Go wherever you wanted. All I would ask in return is that you be available to me when I need you and that you not fuck anyone else."

This guy had some serious balls. He was also a complete idiot. I laughed. "Luca would kill you. You have to know that. And I'm not saying that because I think I'm such a prize or anything, but even I know he's not one to share." I leaned closer, genuinely concerned for him. Notwithstanding his offer to me, he seemed like a nice enough guy.

Scooting his chair closer to me, he picked up my hand and kissed the back of it. "Luca will not be a problem very soon."

It took an act of willpower I didn't know I possessed to keep my expression neutral. "What are you saying?"

But he just took a sip of his wine. "It's nothing you need to worry about. Just know you won't have to worry about him."

I fought the urge to pull my hand from his. "What about my family? My parents?"

"They will be well taken care of. I'll make sure of it."

I pretended to think about it, and then I shook my head. "No, Tony. I'm sorry. Much as I'd like to, I just can't put you in danger like that." *What are you doing, Veda? Leading him on like this. This wasn't me. I'd figure out* another way to get Luca to let me go as soon as my mom was up to traveling. I pulled my hand from his and stood up to take my plate to the sink. "Thank you, though. You're really sweet."

He stood up also, grabbing my arm when I tried went to pick up my dishes. "Hey, just wait a minute."

There was a look in his eyes I didn't like, and when I tried to pull my arm away, he wouldn't let go. "What are you doing?"

"Come on, Veda. Let's just talk about this some more."

I tried to back away, but he followed me until my back was up against the wall. "Tony, stop. You don't want to do this."

"Yeah, I do," he told me. "I've wanted to do this since the first time I saw you."

"If Luca finds out—"

"Luca isn't going to find out."

The finality in his tone is what caught my attention. "What's going on with Luca? Are you planning something with him?"

"Nothing you need to worry about," he said again. His free hand came up to tangle in my hair and he pulled it hard, forcing my face up to his. "I'll take good care of you, Veda. I swear it."

His mouth came down on mine, and my entire body froze for a moment. As his lips moved over mine, trying to get a response out of me, I wasn't repulsed by him. Not at all. But his kiss was strange, and contained none of the soul-wrenching hunger of Luca's kisses. It didn't make my blood surge to the surface of my skin until I thought I would die if he didn't touch me. My heart didn't race one second and stop the next, only to start again as desire tightened low in my stomach and breasts swelled and my pussy clenched in anticipation. His body felt strange against me. He wasn't mine. And I wasn't his.

I pushed against his chest and turned my face away. "Tony, stop. Stop!"

"You should be mine, Veda."

"Except she's not yours. Is she, *stronzo?*"

A bucket of ice over his head wouldn't have had as much of an effect as that cold, lethal voice. Tony stiffened against me, his eyes clashing with mine. The feeling of relief that swept through me shouldn't have come as such a surprise, yet it did. Between one second and the next, tears filled my eyes as I realized I was well and truly lost. I wondered if I'd ever be able to be with another man after Luca.

Completely misconstruing the cause of these tears, Tony dropped a kiss on my temple as my eyes widened in fear for him.

An animalistic growl filled the room, and he was ripped away from me and slammed into the wall beside me. I'd never seen Luca's face so deadly calm. Staring into his friend's eyes, he told him, "You fucking dare to touch her? To kiss her? Right in front of me?? Veda is MINE."

Tony opened his mouth to respond, and I screamed when I saw the flash of Luca's blade, my hands covering my mouth in horror as he buried it to the hilt in Tony's stomach, then sliced him open all the way to his heart. Twisting the knife, he pulled it out and stabbed him again. And again. Until his guts spilled out and blood covered the both of us. Tony's brown eyes glazed over, his mouth still open, about to speak.

Luca stepped back, and Tony's body collapsed to the floor. Bending over him, he cleaned his blade on Tony's pants and put it back in his pocket. Then he calmly walked over to the sink and washed his hands as I stood staring down at the man who had shared dinner with me just a few minutes before.

"What did you do?" I whispered. "Oh my god, Luca. What did you do?"

Enzo walked into the kitchen a few seconds later, and I realized Luca must've texted him. He looked down at the body on the floor and removed his sunglasses. His eyes met mine, and then he pulled out his cell and called someone.

I heard something about needing the kitchen cleaned and not much else, my mind still in shock over the murder I'd just witnessed. "You killed him," I said.

"As I will kill anyone who dares to lay their hands on you," he answered from behind me. I felt the front of him press against my back and his arms slipped around my waist. And even as my mind screamed that he was a cold-blooded killer, that I needed to run, my body sighed into him. "Whatever the fuck you were doing," he said quietly in my ear, "I would suggest you don't try it again. Or this house will be littered with bodies, and I'll have no one left to run security."

He was right. This was completely my fault. Oh my god.

"Now, I hear your father in the other room. Go deal with him while we get this cleaned up."

Still staring down at Tony, I asked, "What do I tell him?"

"Tell him the truth. Or at least the truth, as he needs to know it. Tony was accosting you. And I killed him for it." With one arm still around my waist, he guided me away from the body and out toward the great room where I now saw my father. Tristan stood in front of him, blocking his path so he didn't come any farther. His eyes closed in relief when he saw me, then opened again and immediately fell to my blood-soaked clothes.

Numb with shock, I walked toward him to assure him I was okay.

CHAPTER 18
LUCA

$\mathcal{I}$ regretted the fact that I was forced to kill a man I loved as a friend. Not the way I loved Enzo and Tristan, but a friend, nonetheless. Tony was the one who'd gotten me into the club the day I was shot in broad daylight, and I would always appreciate that. Yet it was quite obvious he had no respect for me. If he had, he never would've laid his hands—or his mouth—on my woman.

And he never would've taken my brother's side.

In the car, heading back home after our delivery was canceled because Rene's cousin wasn't "feeling it," I'd watched on my phone as Veda had invited Tony to stay for dinner. How he'd accepted. And how they'd laughed and talked and drank like old friends. I saw immediately what she was trying to do, and I also saw the moment she changed her mind. My Veda was an open book to me. There was nothing she could hide.

Tony, on the other hand, knew damn well they were on camera. It was the reason he'd been so forward with her. He'd wanted to rub it in my face how easy it had been to steal her away from me. Or so he'd thought. A few weeks ago, I'd started suspecting he was working for Mario. I don't know what he'd offered him, but it was enough to turn one of my most loyal men away from me.

The original plan was to take him out to the garage and get him to tell me what my brother was up to now through whatever means necessary. But that had all changed the moment he pressed my *vita* up against that wall.

"Drop his head off on my brother's doorstep," I instructed Milo.

"You got it." With the body wrapped in a tarp from the garage so it wouldn't drip blood all over the house, Tristan helped him pick it up and take it out to his car. Milo was my cleaner. He would take it off the property and dispose of it. I didn't know how or where, and I didn't care. All I knew was he had worked for me and some other members of the family for years. We paid him well, and not once had the law come knocking on our door. As a matter of fact, not one of the bodies had ever been found. He was fast and efficient, came whenever we needed him, day or night, and looked like a California surfer with his shaggy blond hair cut short on the sides and back, green eyes, and a hoop earring.

When he was gone, we called in some help for Lisa to remove any trace of blood from the walls, floor, table, and chairs. Since I'd used a knife instead of the gun tucked into my pants, it had kept the mess relatively contained. It had also been much more satisfactory for me.

By the time I headed upstairs to shower and change, carrying my shoes and socks so I didn't track anything through the house, Veda's father was back in his room, and she was waiting for me in ours.

She turned from her spot by the doors leading out to the balcony when I came in, staring at me like she didn't know me. "You murdered him. Right in front of me."

I ran my eyes over her. She was covered in blood. "Take off your clothes," I told her.

"He wasn't even armed."

Her face was pale. Too pale. "Veda."

Her eyes shot to my face.

"Your clothes. There's blood on them. Take them off."

She looked down, her eyebrows going up in surprise when she saw all of the blood on her clothes and bare legs. "Oh my god."

Grabbing a plastic bag out of the closet, something I kept there for occasions such as this, I dropped my shoes and socks inside and then took off my jacket and shirt and dropped them in the bag, along with my pants. In only my boxer briefs, I took the bag over to her and set it on the floor by her feet. I'd have to have the cleaning crew come back tomorrow and help Lisa scrub the floor everywhere Veda might have walked.

"Come here, *amore*. Let me help you."

She stood as if in a daze as I took off her shirt and shorts, dropping them into the bag. When I looked up, her gray eyes clashed with mine. "Why did you do that?" she asked me. "Why did you cut him open like that?"

"Because you're mine," I told her simply. "Because it felt good. And I'll do the same to anyone who tries to take you from me."

She searched my face. Always searching. "I'll never be able to leave you, will I?"

I looked her right in the eye. "No, *amore*. Your place is with me now."

"What will you do to keep me with you, Luca?"

"Anything, *amore*. I would do anything."

She hesitated, but only for a second. "Would you kill your own brother?"

The short answer to that would be yes. Of course, I would. I would do it gladly. And not just for her, but for me as well. But at the moment, my hands were tied. I brushed her hair away from her face. "Mario will get what he has coming to him in time. Let's get cleaned up and go to bed. We can talk tomorrow."

But when I went to walk away, she didn't follow me. I stopped and turned around. She stood exactly where I'd left her. "Veda, are you coming?"

Tears filled her eyes and spilled down her cheeks. "No." A sob escaped her, and she covered her mouth with her hand, then hurried to the closet.

I frowned and followed her, watching silently as she grabbed a dark-colored shirt out of her drawer and pulled it on over her bloody bra, then started digging around for a pair of pants. "What are you doing?"

"I can't stay here," she told me. "I can't stay here with you."

Something cold and heavy filled my chest and sank down into my stomach. "You're not going anywhere."

She ignored me, grabbing the black stretchy pants from the night before out of the laundry basket at the back of the closet and slipping them on.

"Veda, did you hear what I said?"

Finding her running shoes, she shoved her feet into them, then walked past me out into the bedroom without looking at me. I followed her.

"Where is my phone?" she asked. But before I could answer her, she walked out of the room, turning right toward her parents' room and leaving the door wide open.

"Goddammit, Veda!" I yelled after her. "You are NOT leaving here."

She disappeared into the guest room, shutting the door behind her.

I stood in the middle of the hall in my underwear, trying to decide if I wanted to barge in after her and carry her out over my shoulder and tie her to the fucking bed or wait until she came out on her own. Either way, she was going to end up in my bed tonight. Where she belonged.

But before I could decide, she came back out and walked right up to me, taking me off guard. "If it's alright, I'll make arrangements to take my parents somewhere else as soon as I can. Is it okay if they stay here until my mother can travel?"

"Veda..."

"Is it okay? Yes or no?"

"Yes, of course."

"Thank you," she told me. I thought she would try to leave then, but once again she surprised me. Setting her jaw, she lifted her chin, even as her eyes filled with fresh tears. "I can't stay here, Luca. You have to let me go."

I shook my head. "No." She was upset by what had happened. I understood that. And I should've waited until she wasn't in the room, but I'd let my anger guide me. "I don't have to do anything."

"You told me I was no longer your prisoner. Were you lying?"

I stared into her gray eyes and felt the ice in my chest harden with every passing second of this conversation. "No. I was not lying."

She looked down at her phone and pulled up her contacts, hitting the button that said, "Sammy." Then, her eyes on mine, she put it up to her ear. "Hey, it's me," she said when her friend answered. "Can you come get me at the marina where you dropped me off?" She paused, and I heard Sammy tell her she would. "Thank you. I'll be there in a few minutes, and I'll wait for you." Another pause. "Okay. See you soon."

"Veda, what are you doing?"

"I'm leaving, Luca. And I'm asking you to *please* let me."

My teeth began to ache, and I realized I was clenching my jaw. "You want to go to your friend's apartment?"

"Yes."

"Why?"

"Because I can't be anywhere near you right now," she told me as her bottom lip trembled and tears slipped down her cheeks. But her voice was strong. Decisive.

I ran my hands through my hair, trying to suppress the scream of rage that was building inside of me. This wasn't happening. This wasn't fucking happening. "Just for tonight."

She spoke so quietly I barely heard her. "Not just for tonight."

"No," I told her. "NO."

"And it's not because of what happened tonight," she went on as if I hadn't spoken. "Not totally."

"I don't fucking understand, Veda."

She glanced down at my bare chest. "Do you want to go talk about this somewhere else?"

"No. We'll talk about it right fucking here. Right fucking now." For once, I had no idea where she was going with this. "Explain this to me, *amore*. I understand what happened tonight was hard for you to witness—"

She held up her hand to stop me. "Luca, I can't live in this world. I don't know the rules."

"I can teach you. Veda, you'll be safe with me. I swear it to you." My anger was beginning to disintegrate into desperation.

"But that's just the thing, Luca. I'll never be safe with you."

I drew back. "What are you talking about? I just killed a man for you."

"You killed a man for daring to touch what you consider yours. And I suspect because you knew he was working for Mario now. As long as your brother is alive, I'll never be safe here. And not just because he's getting to your people. Everything you do is centered around this...competition with Mario. This game you both play. And I'm only a pawn. Something moved around the board at will until I'm captured by one or the other."

"That's not true, *amore*."

She stared up at me, her heart in her eyes. "Prove it to me."

I frowned. "I killed a man for touching you tonight. How much proof do you need?"

But she shook her head. "You killed the wrong man. Tony was only a piece on the board, like me."

Ah. So that's what she was getting at. "Veda, my father put out the order Mario isn't to be harmed. If I go against that order, I won't live long enough to protect you."

"I understand that. I really do." Something inside of me cracked open wide when she gave me a sad smile. "And that's why I'm taking myself off the board." Stretching up on her toes, she took my face in her hands and kissed me hard, her mouth moving on mine until I responded to her. But when I lifted my hands to pull her closer, she broke it off and backed away. She stared up at me for a long moment as tears slid silently down her cheeks, then, without a word, she walked quickly down the hall to the stairs.

I stood frozen as I heard her talking to Enzo. I heard my phone buzz in the bedroom as he texted me. "Take her wherever she wants to go," I called down to him.

And then I went into my room and shut the door as my *vita*, the woman who had become my whole world, walked out of my life.

CHAPTER 19
VEDA

Eight Days Later

The day I walked out of Luca's house was the hardest day I'd ever had in my life, but it was something I'd had to do. I knew that. It had taken me a few days, but I'd finally gotten arrangements made to fly both me and my parents out of the country. I'd spoken to my father every day on the phone, checking on them. And every day he'd told me the same thing, that they were being well taken care of.

I'd also talked my father into coming with me when I left. He'd finally agreed, and I'd located a real estate agent to put their home up for sale and spent the last week packing up more of their things and cleaning it up for photos. Some of it I put in storage, and their luggage I took with me back to Sammy's. We would sell the house with all of the furniture included.

Two days after I'd left Luca's, I realized Enzo was following me everywhere I went. I never said a word to him. Honestly, I was glad for the protection. And when it was time for me to get my parents, he was the one who picked me up at Sammy's just before dinner and brought me back to the lake house.

However, this time when I arrived, Luca was outside waiting for me when I got out of the SUV. I eyed him warily, squinting my eyes against the bright afternoon sun. The air was humid with the promise of rain that would probably never come. "Enzo, what the hell is this?"

Luca approached me from the direction of the garage, and I could see even from where I was in the drive that he was sweating from the heat of late summer. He wore his normal daily attire of black slacks and a white button-down shirt, his sleeves rolled up to his elbows, showing off lean, muscular forearms. But that was where the similarities ended.

His hair was wild, like he'd been combing his fingers through it repeatedly. And his bright blue eyes were crazed, lit from behind by a manic light as they hungrily took in my face, my hair, and then roamed over the rest of my body. I suddenly wished I'd worn more than bike shorts, a gray cotton tee, and sneakers.

Gradually, I noticed there was blood splattered on his face and shirt. And the longer I stared at him, the more injuries I saw. One eyebrow was split open, and his eye was swelling, along with one side of his mouth. His knuckles were swollen, a few of them cut and bloody. And there were dark stains on his pants I assumed was more blood.

He stopped a few feet away, and I took a step forward before I could stop myself, barely resisting the urge to run my hands over him to search for more injuries. My heart thudded hard in my chest, making me a bit lightheaded. Was this even his blood? Or someone else's? But I forced myself not to go any closer. "What happened?" I demanded. "What have you done?"

"I got you a gift, *amore*," he told me. With a nod at Enzo, he turned on his heel and walked into the garage.

Enzo placed a hand on my elbow to lead me inside, but I dug in my heels. "No. No. Enzo, please. I don't want to go in there."

He ignored my pleas, forcing me to put one foot in front of the other on the gravel or be dragged.

We entered the garage through the same door Luca did. Once out of the brightness of the sun, it took a minute for my eyes to adjust to the single dim light bulb that hung from the center of the room. I was reminded of the movies once again. The ones where the bad guys brought someone into a place like this to intimidate them or torture them into making a confession.

But this wasn't the movies. This was real life. And Luca was covered in blood...

As Enzo closed and locked the door behind us, I blinked, and the room slowly came into view. I quickly lowered my eyes and kept them on the floor. I was afraid of what I might see. But I smelled metal and oil. The air was thick with it in the heat and humidity. Too thick. I couldn't seem to get enough oxygen into my lungs and I opened my mouth to take a breath, tasting the copper scent of blood on my tongue. The only sound was from the air conditioning unit running full blast in the far window. It did little to nothing in such a big space.

"Look at what I got for you, *amore*."

But I couldn't. "I don't want anything from you." Spinning around, I tried to leave, but Enzo stuck out his arm and stopped me, then took me by the arms and forced me to turn back around. I could try to fight my way out, but I knew in the end, I didn't have much choice.

"I never took you for a coward, Veda," Luca taunted me. "Open your fucking eyes and see what I brought you."

I tried one more time to reason with him. "Luca, please," I whispered. "Whatever it is. I don't want it. I don't want to see. I just want to go home. And you can do that. I haven't seen anything, so it's okay to let me go." I was rambling, hoping something I said would get through to him.

"OPEN YOUR FUCKING EYES!"

His voice rang through the empty space. Filled with anger and desperation, it echoed off the walls and vibrated through my bones. My eyes flew open.

Luca stood in the middle of the room like a blood-covered, vengeful god. The light bulb swung back and forth over his head, creating light and shadow on his face, turning him into some kind of monster. Not a god. A demon, perhaps. Beside him was a metal chair, and there was a man sitting in it.

Mario.

He was tied to the chair much like Luca had once done to me, only with zip ties instead of silk scarves. I could see where they cut into the skin of his wrists and ankles, his pant legs pulled up so they would be tight. His head was slumped forward on his chest, and the front of his white T-shirt was soaked with blood and plastered to his chest.

Funny, I felt nothing at all seeing him sitting there like that. He'd obviously been beaten. Maybe tortured. But there was just...nothing. No sense of empathy. No anger. Not even a feeling of satisfaction. And when I spoke, my voice was level and even. "Is he dead?"

Luca grabbed him by the hair and yanked his head up. His brother's face was a swollen, bloody mess. Mario's low moan told me that he was, in fact, still alive.

"Oh my god."

"I tied him up after I beat the fuck out of him," Luca told me. "He had a fair chance."

"Why didn't you kill him?" There was genuine curiosity behind my question.

Luca let go of his hair, and Mario's head fell back onto his chest. "I was saving him for you, *amore*."

"And what the fuck do you expect me to do with him?" My stomach rolled, and I thought I was going to be sick.

"Whatever you'd like."

I stared at what was left of the man who'd made my life hell ever since Luca had brought me into their game. "I don't want to do anything with him," I told him. "Can I go home now?"

Luca's mouth twisted and he turned to look down at his brother. "This *pezzo di merda*—this asshole!—killed your sister." His eyes, black in the shadows of his face, caught mine. "He tried to kill your parents. He would've killed you. And me. And you want me to *what?* Let him go?"

As the shock of his appearance began to wear off, something stirred in my gut. He was right. The son of a bitch didn't deserve to be let off easy. But this wasn't me. "Do what you want with him, Luca. But I don't want any part of it."

He swiftly closed the distance between us and grabbed my chin in his bloody hand, forcing me to look at him. "That's not what you want."

I met him look for look. "You don't know what I want."

"Yes. I do."

Something cold and hard touched my hip as he let go of my face. Without thinking, I automatically wrapped my hand around it, feeling cold metal against my palm. I looked down. It was a gun. I shook my head and tried to hand it back to him. "No, Luca. Take it back."

Holding his hands up in front of him, palms toward me, he backed away.

I held it out to him. "I'm not shooting anyone. I can't. Especially not someone who's unconscious."

Luca spun around on his heel and stalked to the back of the garage, where there was a large sink. Turning on the faucet, he filled a bucket full of water and took it back over to his brother, dumping it over his head.

Mario came awake with a jerk, spitting and sputtering. The eye that wasn't swollen shut squinted at me, much like my mother did, then dropped down to the gun in my hand. He burst out laughing, but it was cut off with a groan as he leaned forward and coughed. I would guess he had a few broken ribs. For my father's ribs his men had broken? An eye for an eye, perhaps. When he sat up, his tongue licked at his busted lip before he grinned at me. The same smile he'd given me after he'd sliced his initial into my flesh. My fingers tightened around the pistol in my hand.

He glanced over at his brother. "What the hell do you expect her to do with that?" He jerked his chin at me. "That one doesn't have the balls. She's not near the woman her sister was." He turned his one good eye back to me, then spit a mouthful of blood onto the floor.

"Shut your mouth."

At my words, he gave me a bloody grin. "Why? What are you gonna do? Are you gonna cry? Like you did when I shoved my cock down your throat?"

His head snapped back as Luca's fist connected with his jaw in a burst of violence.

"Luca."

At the sound of my voice, he backed off.

Mario stretched his head on his neck from side to side. "You're just pissed because she liked it," he told Luca.

The letter on my chest began to burn as tears of rage filled my eyes. I was right. I knew it even if I couldn't act on it. Mario would never leave me alone unless he was dead.

"God. You look so much like her, though," he went on as he turned his attention back to me. "But she didn't have your fight. My Nicole was a good girl, right up until I had my gun pointed at her head."

Bile rose in my throat, and my hands began to shake. I didn't want to hear this. He was goading me. Trying to see what I would do. I knew it, but I couldn't force my legs to move.

"Even when I told her to walk away and turn around, so I could see her pretty face, so I could remember her just like that. Her mascara running down her face and her lipstick smeared from my cock." He paused, waiting for a reaction. But he didn't get one. I was frozen. My eyes glued to the bloody mess that used to be his face. "She didn't argue with me. Didn't complain. Didn't beg my forgiveness. She just did whatever the fuck I told her to do." He gazed past me, like he was looking into the past. "She would've been a great wife if she could've just kept her fucking mouth shut."

His eyes snapped back to me so fast I jumped. "But I know where you get your fight from." He spit blood on the floor and smiled. "Your mother. That one has fire. One of these days, I'm going back for her," he told me. His tongue protruded from between his swollen lips, moistening them.

My blood burned in my veins and my vision went red. "You leave my mother the fuck alone!"

"No." He shook his head. "I don't think so. She needs a real man between her legs. Not your pussy of a father. I know my brother has them here. He thinks he can protect them. But I'll find her again. Just like I'll find you." His eyes dropped to my chest. "Mmm. Maybe I'll finish the artwork I started. Carve my entire fucking name into that soft skin of yours. Maybe then you'll know who you belong to."

"I don't belong to anyone but myself," I gritted out. Raising the gun, I pointed it at his head. My hand began to shake.

"You don't have the guts," he sneered.

My finger rested on the trigger. Red hot rage boiled in my blood. I knew if I did this, there was no coming back from it. Mario would be dead, and I'd never be the same.

My sister's ghostly white face floated in the air before me, her lively blue eyes dull in death. Memories of my father, beaten and broken. And of my mother, spewing her hate at me like it was my fault Mario had gone after them. If it wasn't for this piece of shit in front of me, my sister would still be alive, ordering me around and my parents would be home. Safe.

And I never would've been taken. I would still be the girl I was before I'd been forced into this sick game.

I took a deep breath. And when I released it, I tightened my finger on the trigger. The gun went off, and the bullet grazed the side of his face.

Mario's eye widened in shock. And then he laughed, loud and crazy.

Hot, angry tears filled my eyes until I couldn't see. I pulled the trigger again. And again. I pulled it over and over until the laughter stopped and Mario's head fell back, his mouth hanging open as his dead eyes stared up at the ceiling. There wasn't much left of his face, although a few shots had hit him in the chest.

I stared at him for a long time, the gun still pointed at his face, until my arm began to tremble violently, and I couldn't hold it up anymore. I dropped the gun to my side and bent at the waist, screaming at the dead body in front of me. I screamed with all of the rage and sorrow inside of me. I screamed in horror. And I screamed in triumph.

And when I was done, when there was nothing left but a comfortable numbness, I breathed. Just breathed. Straightening up, my eyes found Luca and my stomach rolled. I was going to be sick.

Walking over to me, he lifted one hand and cupped my face in his palm. I thought he would take the gun from me then, but he didn't. Instead, he lowered himself to his knees on the blood-covered cement floor.

"What are you doing?" My voice was hoarse from screaming. Tears and snot ran down my face as my entire body trembled with the gravity of what I'd just done.

"I'm giving you a chance, *amore.*"

I stared down at him, confused.

Enzo appeared beside me. I hadn't even realized he was still here. "Luca, what are you doing?"

"What I should've done all along," Luca told him. His blue eyes never left me. "I'm giving Veda a choice."

"Luca, stop it." But even as I said the words, my finger twitched on the trigger.

"If you want to be rid of me, *amore*, this is the only way that's ever going to fucking happen. You can pull that fucking trigger, and you'll be free. Or you can put down the gun. But if you choose the second option, you'll never be able to escape me. I'll hunt you down to the last corners of this fucking earth, and I'll rip apart anyone who tries to keep you from me. So, my *vita*, you have a choice. And this is the only time I'll give it to you." Then he sat back on his heels, placed his palms on his hard thighs, and waited.

Fucking hell, he was offering me a way out.

There was a burning knot in my chest that rose to clog my throat as ragged sobs tore through me. All I'd wanted these last few weeks was to get away from this man and everything he stood for. Yes, he'd fucked me like I'd never been fucked before. He'd protected me. He'd loved me.

But he'd also ripped me from my life. He'd used me, He'd played me. He'd sucked me into his fucking game and tore me open, just to patch me back together again and send me sprawling back out into a world I no longer knew. And I was so fucking done.

Lifting the gun, I pressed the barrel against his forehead. There wouldn't be any missing this time. "I love you," I whispered brokenly.

"I know," he whispered back.

The last thing I heard was Enzo's shout.

And then I pulled the trigger.

CHAPTER 20
LUCA

There was a click, but I didn't flinch. I knew the gun was out of bullets. She'd emptied them all into Mario.

Veda stared down at me with horror in her wide, gray eyes. Then I watched as they filled with new tears. Her face crumpled, and the gun clattered to the floor as she fell into my open arms.

I caught her and pulled her onto my lap as she wrapped her arms around my neck. I held her tight as great heaving sobs wracked her body and she kept repeating my name over and over in terrified, keening cries. I adjusted her legs until they straddled mine and tightened my hold on her, my voice thick with my own tears as I told her, "Shhh...*amore*. It's okay. I'm here."

I felt Enzo's hand squeeze my shoulder, and then heard his footsteps as he left us. At the door, he stopped. "Don't ever *fucking* do that again, Luca." Then he left, shutting the door behind him.

"Are we even now, *amore?*" I whispered near her ear. "Are we done? I tried to kill you. You tried to kill me. Can I love you now? Will you let me?"

She didn't respond. She couldn't. She was crying too hard.

I needed to get her away from all of this blood and death. Without releasing her, I rose to my feet, keeping one arm around her back and one under her sweet ass. Adrenaline still flooded my system. So much I was shaking. Her legs wrapped around my waist as I stood. We were still like that when I took her into the house and up the stairs to our bedroom and straight into our shower.

Hanging onto Veda with one arm, I turned on the faucet and gave the water a few seconds to warm up as I hugged her to me. The hard sobs that had burst from her had subsided into normal sniffles that were no less heart-wrenching to hear. I held her tight. "I'm never letting go of you again, *amore.* Do you hear me?"

Fully clothed, I walked us both into the shower and got under the warm spray. As I started to relax, my arms and legs began to give, and I put my back to the glass wall, then slid down to sit on the tiles with Veda on my lap. I tilted her face back and let the water wash over us. Blood and tears ran down the drain, taking with it everything that had brought us to this point. This was a new start for us. A new beginning. "I love you," I told her.

The water calmed her hysteria, and when she looked at me, I saw no storms in her bloodshot, gray eyes, only disbelief. "I tried to shoot you," she choked out.

"You did." I pushed her wet hair back from her face.

"Luca...I tried to *shoot* you."

Her face crumbled again, and I had to force her to look at me. "Veda. My *vita*. Look at me, *amore*. Hey. Hey. LOOK at me."

But when she did as I asked, I had no words. No way to tell her all that I was feeling. Hell, I didn't even fucking know. So I tightened my hold on her precious face and brought her lips to mine, taking her mouth like that kiss was my last breath.

I kissed her hungrily. Desperately. The shower spraying over our heads. And something deep inside of me began to realize there was a chance I never would've kissed her again. What if I'd miscounted the bullets? What if Mario had gotten to her before I'd gotten to him?

Pain lanced through me in white hot bursts, and I choked it down, telling myself it was okay. She was here. And so was I. I felt her under my hands. Tasted her with my tongue. Felt her weight on my lap, her pussy pressing against my swollen cock, and my hands went to the waistband of her shorts, tearing at the fastenings. "Take these off," I ordered, my voice rough with my own tears. "Now."

I watched as her hands replaced mine. They were shaking so much I thought I'd have to rip the fucking things from her, but she eventually got it. I helped her get up on her knees and pull them down over her hips and one leg until her foot was free and she was back on my lap in nothing but cotton panties, a bra, and a wet T-shirt. I pulled it up and over her head, and then we were kissing again, and her moans were in my ears as I rolled my hips into the heat of her body.

But it wasn't enough. It was never enough with her. Breaking off the kiss, I ripped the button from my pants as I struggled to get them undone one-handed. As soon as my cock was free, I pulled her panties to the side and slid inside of her, both of us crying out as she tightened around me, all wet heat and trembling limbs.

"*Fuck*...Veda..." Her name ended on a moan as we sat there wrapped around each other, unmoving except for our chests lifting up and down with each breath. I was so deep inside of her I could feel her womb, and yet I wanted to be closer still. I wanted to crawl inside of her and wrap her around me until I felt her blood pulse through my veins and her soul caress mine. I lifted her so that I slid halfway out, then pulled her back down. The feel of her skin. The scent of her sex. The sound of her soft cries. They echoed around me in the shower as she took me so deep my eyes rolled back in my head.

"Luca...I need you to fuck me." The order was low and sexy in my ear, almost timid, and it fucking undid me. Bending my knees, I used my hands on her hips to guide her as I picked up speed, torn between the raw lust of my body and the need to never have this end. I felt myself sliding on the wet tiles and went with it, lying flat on the shower floor as this woman, this fucking stunning, beautiful, brave woman, braced her hands on my chest and threw her head back until the water sprayed over her and onto me. She rocked her hips, seating herself fully, and I cursed softly at the tightness of her around my cock, her ass on my thighs and her fragile hands holding me captive beneath her more effectively than the heaviest chains ever could.

I let her set the pace, fast and hard, the contrast of her near naked body sitting atop my fully dressed form one of the hottest fucking things I'd ever seen in my life. Her head fell forward, water running over the back of her head to drip down her hair and wet the front of her bra until it was nearly transparent. I reached for one breast, hefting the weight in my palm and feeling the nipple harden beneath my thumb through the thin material.

Then I dropped my hand back down to her hip as my orgasm slid down my spine and tightened my balls. I increased the pace, slamming into her sweet body. "Come with me, *vita*."

"Luca." She cried out my name, her hands going to her breasts as she let me take control.

"Ah, god. *Fuck...*" My thumb found her clit, swollen and hard, and as soon as I touched her, she stiffened over me. "Holy *fuck,*" I repeated as my orgasm hit me. My eyes went wide, watching her face as I cried out her name, pulling her down until I was as deep as I could go, filling her with my come. With the very essence of me.

Her chest and neck flushed red as she shuddered over me, the scar my brother made white in contrast, and I felt her pussy pulse around my cock, milking me for all I was worth. Reaching up with both hands, I grabbed her head and pulled her mouth down to mine, needing the connection as I came down. She came willingly, collapsing on top of me.

The kiss went from something wild and uncontrolled to calm, lazy strokes of my tongue inside her mouth, then easy brushes of my lips against hers. I nipped her bottom lip just before I let her pull away.

She tucked her face into my neck, and I wrapped my arms around her as we laid there on the shower floor with me still inside of her.

"I love you, *amore,*" I told her again. "Will you stay with me now?" I would call Milo to take care of my brother and pay him five times his normal rate to keep his mouth shut about it. As far as my father needed to know, he'd just disappeared again. He couldn't suspect a thing, ever, or I was as good as dead. And so was Veda.

She lifted her head just enough to look down at me. Her wet hair was plastered to her cheeks, her eyes were red and puffy from crying, and her lips were swollen from my kisses. I'd never seen anyone more beautiful in my life. "Luca, this is so fucked up."

"Do you love me?" I asked her.

My heart stopped when she wouldn't answer me. Instead, she pulled away from me and sat up, shoving her wet hair out of her face. "Do you not see how fucked up this is?"

"Why?" I asked her. "Because it's not what you see in the movies? Or read about in books? This is life, Veda. It's my life. And I want you in it. Every day. Every fucking hour." I sat up, my ribs screaming at me where Mario had kicked me. "I can't promise you normal. I'll never be able to give you a white picket fence. But whether you like it or not"— I caught her eyes with mine—"you're mine now, Veda. I told you when I gave you that gun and knelt in front of you that killing me was the only way you would ever get rid of me."

Her expression was unreadable. "But I did try to kill you."

She did. But she was emotional then. Not thinking straight. I searched her eyes as she did mine. Always searching. But this time, I let her see. I let her see it all. My love. My fear. My obsession.

Lifting her leg away from my hip, I dug into the front pocket of my wet pants, pulled out my knife and opened it, then handed it to her handle first. "You want to be rid of me, *amore?* This is your final chance." Taking her hand that held the knife, I aimed the blade at my heart, then took her other hand and pressed that around it too. "Contrary to what they show you in the movies, it's actually kind of difficult to sever someone's jugular in their throat. However, if you push down here"—I tapped my chest right next to the point of my blade—"and put your body weight behind it, that blade will slide right into my heart. Even if you bounce off a rib and miss, it will most likely enter a lung, which will then fill with blood until I drown in it."

She stared down at my face, her hands gripping the knife, my cock still inside of her. Her eyes flicked down to my chest and back to my face.

"If you want your freedom, *amore*, you have a second chance. Right now. All you have to do is push. Then get up and walk away." I let my arms fall to my sides. If she pushed that blade in, it wouldn't be the knife that killed me. My heart would shatter all on its own.

Long seconds passed with only the sound of the shower to break the silence.

Then Veda tilted her head, and her eyes fell to the front of my shirt. Still holding the knife in one hand, she unbuttoned it as far as she could and spread the material wide until my bare chest was exposed. She took a quick glance at my face before her eyes fell back to my chest.

I knew immediately what she wanted to do. What she needed. And I would give her anything to lessen the hurt inside of her. I would let her peel the skin from my body piece by piece. "Do it," I told her.

She started to shake her head, and then stopped. Her eyes fell to my chest again.

"Do it," I repeated.

With a shaking hand, she put the point of the knife at the bottom of my right collarbone. And that was where she stayed.

Wrapping my hand around hers, I pressed until I felt it puncture my skin, then I guided her hand, dragging it down to the center of my breastbone. Pain lanced through me, and it was fucking glorious. My blood began to race, and my cock swelled inside of her until it was so hard her muscles clenched around me. Water from the shower made the open wound burn and washed away the blood as fast as it flowed. Moving her hand to the other side, I helped her carve another line that joined the first. When we were done, there was a "V" carved into my chest.

The knife clattered to the tile floor, and I caught her face in my hands as she leaned forward to kiss me. I tasted her tears, and swallowed her moans as she began to rock her hips. "Now you are mine, Luca," she whispered against my lips. "*Mine...*"

"Always, *amore*. I'm yours, and only yours. Always..."

EPILOGUE
ENZO

I kicked the front door closed and pressed my back against it, ripping off my sunglasses and taking a minute to breathe. Just fucking breathe. Luckily, no one was around to see the way my eyes skittered wildly around the great room. My heart slammed in my chest, and for a minute I thought it was gonna bust right out of my fucking rib cage. Or I was gonna pass out. One of the two. Or both.

What in the *fuck* had Luca been thinking.

Jesus Christ. If Tristan had been in that garage when he pulled that shit, he would've fucking *lost* it. And I don't know that we would've been able to bring him back. At least not easily.

And Veda...

What the fuck was he trying to do to her? She was a strong woman, but she hadn't grown up around this shit like Luca did. Like Tristan and I did.

The room began to swim, and a drop of sweat trickled down the side of my face. I flexed my hands, spreading my fingers, then closing them again, feeling the tendons stretch. Closing my eyes, I concentrated on my breaths. In, out. In, out. Slow and steady. I felt my lungs expand and my heartbeat slow, little by little, until it was beating normally again and the pain in the center of my chest faded away.

"Enzo? You alright?"

I opened my eyes and met Tristan's concerned stare. "I'm good," I told him. "Everything is good." Then I put my sunglasses back on before he could see the remnants of panic in my eyes. "I think Luca and Veda are working things out."

"He finished off Mario?"

"Yes. He'll no longer be an issue."

Tristan nodded. "Good. It was pure luck I found him alone last night. There's no way Luigi will be able to pin his disappearance on Luca."

I fell into step beside him as we headed into the kitchen to get some coffee. Thank god for Lisa. She always had some ready for us. "We're still gonna have to watch our backs, though. Just in case."

"So same as always, then."

"Yes. Same as always." I touched his shoulder, but only briefly. Not because I didn't feel affection for my lifelong friend, but because he had a difficult time accepting it.

One Week Later

I frowned as Luca joined me at the pool for a late summer swim instead of our usual workout. "What is that?"

Luca glanced down at the bright red "V" carved into his bared chest and smiled. "Penance for my sins. And proof of my loyalty," he answered.

He met my stare proudly, without shame. I just laughed a little and shook my head. And to think, of the three of us, Luca was the one who was the least fucked up.

I'd first noticed the wound when we were sparring together in the gym. Then, for about a week afterward, it remained fresh, sometimes bleeding through his T-shirt because he refused to cover it. I'd thought maybe he'd received it when he'd gotten into it with Mario, so I hadn't asked about it. But now I could clearly see what it was.

And it explained the way Veda often looked at him now with a mixture of horror and possession every time I was with her and Luca walked into the room.

Once, I saw them together in the hall outside of his room. Her hand was lifted, like she wanted to touch his chest, but she stopped before she could, her pretty features twisting into something I couldn't quite read. But before she could lower it again, Luca grabbed her hand and pressed it against the center of his chest, right over the place where the two lines connected; I could see now. It had to have hurt like a bitch, but he'd only smiled and leaned over to gently kiss her mouth.

Not wanting to invade their privacy, I turned away.

The first few nights after Veda took out Mario, I heard her wake up screaming once or twice a night while I kept watch in the house. I was glad her parents had used the plane tickets she'd gotten them and were no longer here. It would've been awful for them to hear that shit. But if she still had nightmares after that, I didn't hear her. And for that, I was grateful. The screaming brought back memories I'd just as soon forget.

Three Months Later

I stood at the open window in Luca's office and took a deep breath. We were in that time of year where Texas was having a hard time letting go of the heat of summer, even though it was almost the holidays, but today the temperature had only gotten up into the sixties. And now that the sun was about to go down, if you took the time to notice, you'd taste the slightest bite of winter in the air and feel the chill linger in your lungs.

Veda was walking the path toward the lake below me, her blond hair blowing in the breeze as she looked out over the water. She was adapting to her life as the girlfriend of a mafia underboss like she'd been born in our world. Luca had brought in a shrink for her to talk to, and if she was still haunted by everything that had happened since she'd met him, I didn't see any signs of it. Except, maybe once in a while, when I'd catch her staring off into space when she thought no one was watching her. But she was even going back to school part-time, taking college courses at the local university with me or Tristan as her constant bodyguard, although Luca went with her when he could. Just the required core courses for now while she decided what she wanted to do with her life.

I'd never seen Luca so content. I was really happy for him. For both of them.

"Enzo, would you close the window, please?"

Looking over my shoulder, I saw Luca come in with Tristan behind him. I closed and locked the window as Luca sat down behind his desk and Tristan took the bag of money he was holding over to the secret panel in the wall that contained the safe. "Everything go okay?" I asked. They'd done the pickup without me, as they'd done ever since the incident with Mario because Luca refused to leave Veda in the house without protection and he'd told me I was the only one he trusted to keep her safe besides Tristan, who he needed with him.

Apparently, the fucking army of men outside the house wasn't enough for him.

"Yeah, it went fine," Luca told me. "Even my father was more mellow than usual. It makes me fucking nervous." As though he could sense her there, he suddenly turned and looked out the window. "How's my *vita* been while I was gone?"

I joined him, sitting in one of the chairs on the other side of the desk. "Good. She's been doing homework and just stepped out to get some air. I've had eyes on her the entire time."

He hesitated for a moment, and I knew he wanted to call her back into the house.

"Let her get some air, Luca. She'll be okay for a few minutes."

After another few seconds, he turned back around, but spun his chair to the side so he could keep an eye on her while we talked. "The annual fundraiser is coming up," he said as Tristan sat down beside me. "The family needs to make an appearance, and I'd like you both there with me."

"Of course," Tristan told him. "As long as I don't need to bring anyone."

The corners of Luca's mouth turned up just slightly. "It's not a requirement. You can come solo."

"Perfect."

Speaking of which. "Do you need me for anything else tonight?" I asked Luca.

He shook his head. "Not until later. You should get some sleep."

"Yeah." I stood up. "Do you want me to call Veda in before I go?"

But Luca's attention was already back outside with her. "No. I've got her. I'll see you later tonight."

Slapping palms with Tristan, I took my leave, checking the time on my cell phone. I had a date to keep myself.

And she didn't take kindly to me being late.

Thank you so much for reading Luca and Veda's story! I hope you enjoyed it. And don't worry, we're just getting started.
His Promise, book 1 of Enzo's story, is coming this winter and is available for preorder HERE.

Love,
Angel

And while you wait, check out
Be With Me by Angel Rayne
A Standalone Novel
(Keep reading for a free preview)

I'm not her knight in shining armor. I'm
her downfall. She just doesn't know
it yet.

*When I'm not in school, I make extra cash
working as a model.
My favorite photographer to work with?
Ailee Walsh.
And not just because she's so sexy she
should be in the shots with me.
Although that reason is definitely up
there.
With her dark hair and white skin, Ailee
reminds me of a princess.
The woman makes my head swim and my
stomach tangle up in ropes.
Not to mention what she does to other
parts of me...
The last time I saw her, she was married.
So I did my job and left.
However, I never stopped thinking about
her. Not once.*

Now, a year later, the ring on her finger is
　　gone.
There's nothing stopping me from going
　　after what I want.
Not even the destructive road my life
　　is on...

Being with Ailee would be like a
　　fairytale.
Too bad I'm no fucking prince.

Read Be With Me HERE

PROLOGUE

Tyler

Eight Months Ago

I blinked against the bright glare of a streetlight, gagging on the stench in the air. When my eyes adjusted and I could focus, I looked around, trying to figure out where the fuck I was.

There was a hard brick wall digging into my back where I was slumped against it, and in front of me was some sort of large metal container. Bags that reeked like rotten food and God knew what else overflowed the top and hid me from anyone who might happen to come along.

I took stock of my body, searching for injuries. I felt a little beaten up, but otherwise, I seemed to be okay. When I could manage it, I crawled out of the piles of trash. It was dark, the alley lit only by that damn streetlight. I felt around in my pockets for my cell phone. I had no fucking idea what time it was, or even what day. What I did know was my head felt like it was about to explode, and I hoped like hell no one I knew would see me like this. I had no recollection of going out, or of drinking, but if the taste of death in my mouth was any indication, that's exactly what I'd been doing.

Shaken up, more than a little disoriented, and still searching for my phone, I wracked my brain trying to remember what the fuck had happened. But nothing came to me. It was like I'd lost time somehow. My heart began to pound and a sheen of sweat broke out across my skin despite the cool temperature. I was fucking terrified, my pulse rising to near heart attack levels, when this little tan dog came trotting up to me with his tail wagging and his tongue hanging out of his mouth.

He looked so happy to see me, greeting me like he'd been waiting for me for hours, that I forgot my own issues, if only for a moment or two. I looked around again, expecting his owner to come around the corner looking for him, but no one ever did. I checked for a collar, but he had no tags.

I bent over to pet him, and as I rubbed his soft head, I sagged against the side of the building. Gradually, the pounding in my ears began to slow to a more normal beat.

Dogs, man. We didn't deserve them.

After a while, I tried to get him to go home, assuring him I had nothing on me he would want. He didn't seem to believe me, though, so eventually I gave up trying to convince him to leave and just let him hang out. Patting down my pockets and kicking the trash around on the ground, I tried one more time to find my phone, but it wasn't on me. And I had no idea where I'd left it.

With a groan, I looked down at the dog. "What the actual fuck happened here?" I asked him.

He cocked his head but seemed as clueless as I was.

I pressed the heels of my hands against my pounding temples. My voice sounded like I'd been screaming all night and my eyes burned like hell, so I closed them as I tried to get my shit together. When I opened them again, my new friend was still there. "I feel like shit," I told him.

The dog tilted his head to the other side this time, like he was listening to what I was saying. Then he ran off. I thought maybe he'd finally came to his senses and realized I had no food for him. But a few seconds later, he was back.

With a Snickers bar in his mouth.

Full-sized, too. None of that bite-sized crap.

He dropped it at my feet and barked. I eyed up the candy through eyes that were squinted against the pain in my head, and my stomach growled like I hadn't eaten in a week. And for all I knew, I hadn't. But still... "Sorry, man. I appreciate the offer, but I don't know where you got that or what might be in it. So, I'm gonna pass."

I left the candy bar there. To my right, I saw a street, and I staggered in that direction. Above me, thunder rattled the sky, and I covered my ears in an effort to keep my head from pounding along with the wheels of the light rail. When I made it to the end of the alley, I could see I was in a bad area of Belltown. Okay. I made my way down the main street until I could flag down a taxi to take me home. Luckily, my wallet was still in my back pocket.

The pup followed me out to the road, sitting beside me as I waited for my ride like he belonged there. And when the taxi pulled over, he let out this pathetic little whine, giving me the biggest, saddest, puppy dog eyes I'd ever seen in my life.

I eyed him as I stood there with the back door open. I wanted to help him, but as I was recently discovering I could barely take care of myself.

However, at the thought of leaving him there and heading home to spend the rest of the night alone, my heart picked up again, beating so fast and hard I swayed on my feet.

Finally, I took a deep breath and gave in. "You wanna come?"

That was all the invitation he needed. With a happy grin on his furry face and his tongue lolling out, he hopped into the back, sitting on the seat like he did this sort of thing all the time. Climbing in behind him, I gave the driver directions to my apartment, and we went home.

Later the next day, I found out I'd been MIA for two days.

This was the first time that had ever happened to me. I lost five more days and spent hundreds on doctor copays over the next three months, trying to figure out why I couldn't remember going out or why I would black out when I didn't remember drinking. I was tested for every physical ailment under the sun. No one could tell me what had happened, or why, and eventually, I just gave up.

Determined not to spend my life agonizing over a few weird days, I pushed the memories—or lack thereof—to the back of mind and forgot about them.

Not so much the dog, though.

Nah. He stayed with me.

.   .   .

Chapter 1

Tyler

I was going to see Ailee again. After almost a year, I was finally going to see her again. And honestly, I wasn't quite sure how I felt about it.

Excited, for sure. Scared? Yeah, a little. Hungry?

Fuck yes.

But not in a cannibalistic kind of way. I'm not a psycho. However, Ailee Walsh was—hands down—one of the most delicious women I'd ever had the honor of meeting. She was...everything. Just fucking everything. Her sparkling eyes were as blue as a cloudless sky, and the way they danced when she laughed made me think of the warm, carefree summer days I'd seen in movies, but I'd never had the opportunity to experience. Not even when I was a kid.

She also had a smile that made my heart pound in my chest. And a voluptuous, old Hollywood figure that girls —and a lot of guys—these days just didn't appreciate. It wasn't their fault. Every fucking media outlet out there told them the only way they'd be attractive was to be as thin and wafer-like as possible.

But me? I was a man who liked a woman that filled up the space between my arms. A woman I could sink into and lose myself in without worrying about breaking one of her fragile bones.

God, I sounded like a fucking Hallmark commercial. And I probably looked like I belonged in one as I stared out my kitchen window, the perfect picture of one of the characters in those movies my mom was always watching. But as cheesy as I sounded, even to myself, it was all true, what I thought about her. Hell, I was getting hard just thinking about it.

And, I'd just heard she'd recently gotten divorced.

Something cold and wet hit the back of my knee, bringing my thoughts back to the fact that I had a modeling appointment with Ailee, the only photographer I've ever felt self-conscience around. With a shaking hand, I set down my new cell phone on the counter and found Snickers sitting behind me. I gave him a smile, leaning over to rub his long, soft ears. "Hey, buddy. Where ya been?" My dog licked my hand as I tried to brush dirt from his creamy white muzzle.

My phone chimed again, and I gave my pup one last pat before I straightened up to see a text from Stefanie, the romance author who'd just booked me for her new cover. She said she'd heard back from Ailee and we were good to go for the date she'd told me, exactly two weeks from now. I texted her back, thanking her for thinking of me and assuring her I had it on my calendar and that I would be there.

There was no fucking way I would miss it. And not just because I desperately needed the money.

Phone still in my hand, I sat down hard, nearly missing the chair I'd yanked out from beneath the kitchen table. A shiver ran over me, and it had nothing to do with the fact that I was wearing nothing but dark blue boxer briefs. My first-floor apartment was warm, but I refused to turn on the A/C. It was nearly fall, the weather should be cooling down by now, and I wasn't about to blow money I didn't have on a high electric bill.

Glancing at the time on the microwave, I took a steadying breath and got my ass in gear. I was supposed to be at that new restaurant near Pike Place in thirty minutes, and I didn't think the restaurant would let Willow hold our table if I wasn't there. I threw on a nice shirt and a pair of jeans, tugged my cleanest pair of sneakers on, and searched frantically for my wallet. I found it on the counter and shoved it and my phone into my back pockets. I wasn't worried about leaving Snickers, he was already curled up in his favorite spot on the couch by the time I left. I closed the patio door that I normally left open for him so he could go muck around in the courtyard at will, smiling at the sound of his soft snores, and then I locked him in and went to go meet my foster sister.

She was already there when I arrived, standing near the door. Tall and slender, she reminded me very much of her namesake with her pale skin, and her light-colored hair that rose from her scalp and dangled in wispy curls just past her shoulders. "Hey." I greeted her with a kiss on the cheek. "Sorry, the bus was running late."

My excuse was met with the "arched brow of disbelief" and blank stare I'd been receiving since we were kids. "More like you forgot about our date until the last minute, then you threw on the first shirt you found in your closet, grabbed a pair of jeans from the semi-clean pile, and ran out the door."

I grinned at her.

"Did you at least feed Snickers before you left?"

"Nah," I told her. "He was snoring on the couch when I left. I'll feed him when I get home."

"Don't forget, you still need to get me a key," she reminded me as the hostess led us to our table.

I had forgotten. But it was no big deal. We always had keys to each other's place, ever since we'd both moved to Seattle. I'd agreed it was a good idea. It was just easier if either one of us had to pet sit or whatever, even though her damn cat still didn't like me. "I've only been in the new apartment a few weeks. I'll get one made this weekend."

I opened the menu the hostess had given us and started checking out what was there. The place looked like a fusion of Mexican food and Thai food. Interesting. The waiter came over and I ordered an iced tea, then went back to studying the menu.

"All right. What's up with you?"

I looked at Willow over the top of my menu. "Me?"

She rolled her eyes. "Yeah, you. Either your leg is possessed, or you've suddenly got some kind of major nervous tick. You're jostling the whole table, Ty, and you haven't sat still for two seconds since you got here. So, what's up?"

I hid behind my menu again. We'd known each other most of our lives. There was no way I'd be able to look her in the eye and deny I was nervous. And I could say for certain that it wasn't going to get any better as the day I was going to see Ailee again got closer and closer. And that right there was ammunition my sister did NOT need to know. "Nothin'. I got a call for a shoot right before I came here. I'm just a little nervous."

My menu was yanked from my hands and slapped down flat onto the table. "Bullshit. You never get nervous about shoots. And this is how I know you're lying to me. Which you also can't do well. So, you might as well fess up now."

I grinned at her. I couldn't help it. "Or, what? You'll call Mom and tell on me?"

She smiled sweetly for a brief second, right before she whipped out her cell phone from her purse and made like she was doing exactly that.

I laughed. "Knock it off. You know damn well you're not calling anyone."

Willow turned the phone around so I could see. The word "Mom" and our foster mother's phone number lit up the screen, and it was ringing. I tried to grab it from her, but she pulled it away just in time. "You're such a fucking brat." I laughed.

"Hi, Mom!" she said a moment later. I could hear our foster mother's southern drawl on the other end. Willow winked at me. "I'm good." She paused as the woman, who was our mother for all intents and purposes, fired off the usual questions. "Yeah, I'm still working at the craft shop. Nope, still not dating anyone." Another pause. "Because I'm tired of men and all the girls at work are straight." She grinned at me. "So, Tyler's here. Uh huh. Yup." Her face screwed up in thought. "I'm not sure." She dragged out the words, adding a touch of drama to her show. "He seems to be okay, but he's really nervous about something and won't tell me what it is." Another pause. "Sure. Okay. Yup. Love you, too." With a look of triumph, she held the phone out to me.

I made no move to take it. "Really?" I asked her.

"Tyler, you better pick up the phone." Our mother's laughing voice could barely be heard above the energetic music playing through the speakers in the ceiling.

I rolled my eyes, much to Willow's amusement, and took the phone from her outstretched hand. "Hi, Mom."

"Honey, why do you tease your sister like that?"

"Because it's fun." I stuck my tongue out at Willow like I used to do when we were younger. She was a few years older and came from a completely different background. But once we'd both gotten comfortable in our new home, we'd grown up just like any two siblings. And that included me getting away with murder while she got stuck cleaning the house—when she wasn't bogged down with homework, anyway. Willow had taken all advanced classes through high school and college, graduating with a double major in law and political science. So why she worked in a craft store was a mystery none of us knew the answer to.

I chatted with my foster mother, not realizing until just this moment how much I'd missed her and our foster dad. They lived in the northern part of Texas near Amarillo, and that's where we'd grown up. As the only two kids in the house, my sister and I had grown close. When I'd decided to move to Seattle a few years ago, Willow had decided to come with me. We'd roomed together for the first year, until she met her ex-boyfriend and moved in with him, leaving me with the apartment all to myself. After they broke it off, she chose to stay on her own, although she was never very far away. And out of necessity, I'd found a smaller, cheaper apartment near Pioneer Square. I'd just got settled in right before I found Snickers. It was good that my new place allowed pets.

After reassuring my mom that all was okay and catching her up on what was happening in my life—at least the happy, abbreviated version—I hung up right as the waitress showed up to take our orders. "I can't believe you did that to me," I shot at her when we were alone again.

Willow wasn't affected by my attempt at anger. She waved a hand in the air. "Pfft. Whatever. You need to call home more."

She was absolutely right. However, that wasn't the point. "You're lucky we're in a public place."

"Or what?" Her eyes narrowed, and she was once again the ten-year-old girl who'd dared me to stop her from snooping through my stuff.

I shook my head, fighting the urge to smile. I was unable to stay upset with the only stable person in my life. "Don't you have someone else to harass?"

"Nope," she answered cheerfully. "Just you."

"Great." I sighed dramatically.

"So, who are you shooting for?"

I rubbed the back of my neck. "Uh, that author Stefanie Heathers."

"Didn't you work with her before?"

"Yeah, last year." I looked around the restaurant, checking out the other patrons and the décor, hoping like hell she'd drop it. "Have you heard from the loser again?"

Hazel eyes that tilted up at the corners, accentuated by eyeliner, narrowed in on me again. She completely ignored my question about her ex. "You really are nervous about this shoot." Resting her arms on the table, she leaned in. "The question is, why? I know it's not the author. Or what she plans to do with your photo. You've been on lots of romance covers."

"Let it go, Willow."

Again, she completely ignored me. Per the usual. "Who's the photographer?"

The back of my neck burned, and I rubbed it again. "I don't know. Who cares?"

A look of satisfaction crossed her face, and she sat back in her chair. "Well, as I know for a fact that you're completely straight, there's only one female photographer —that I know of—that you've worked with before, and that's the chick who did the last cover Stefanie Heathers wanted, isn't it?"

"She's not a 'chick,' Willow. She's a professional photographer."

"I'm right! Aren't I? It's the photographer chick you're nervous about seeing!" She practically crowed with delight at figuring me out.

I threw up my hands. "Fine. Yes. Okay? Are you happy now?"

All signs of teasing fell from her face. "Are you going to ask her out?"

"No!" Then I shrugged. "I don't know. Maybe." At the thought of being alone with Ailee, my blood raced through my body until I felt lightheaded. I looked at my sister and dropped all sense of pretense. It was no use anyway. "She's not like other women." I didn't know how else to explain it.

"Is she single?"

"I think so, yeah. I heard she just got divorced by one of the other cover models who called me for a reference a few weeks ago."

"Divorced? Already?" She frowned. "How old is she?"

"I don't know. In her early forties. Forty-five, maybe?"

Willow stared at me, her face carefully blank. "That's a big age difference, Ty."

I stared hard at her as the waitress set our orders on the table, silently asking her what the hell that had to do with anything.

"Don't look at me like that," she said once she'd thanked her, and we were alone again.

"It's like ten years. Tops." I picked up my fork. "And even if it's more, or less, who the hell cares? It's not like we're in high school. I don't see why it would matter at this point in our lives."

Willow took a bite of her food, but her attention was still focused on me. I felt her disapproval like a weight on my shoulders. And I totally didn't understand why it was there. I put my fork down without tasting anything, my appetite suddenly gone. Jesus Christ. I wasn't a fucking kid anymore. "What." The word came out harsher than I'd intended. I loved Willow like she was blood, but I was so tired of her mothering me. She'd done it our entire lives, and recently, it had gotten much more intense. I was a grown ass man, for God's sake.

"Don't be mad, Ty. I just worry about you. I want you to be happy. And this woman is just...I don't think she's for you."

"You've never even met her," I ground out. Why I was letting her get under my skin, I didn't know. But she was. My head was beginning to pound from this conversation.

"It's just that she's so much older than you. And divorced? You know there's gotta be baggage there. Does she have kids? How old are they? Is her ex-husband still around?"

I put my elbows on the table and rubbed my temples. "Fuck, Willow. I don't know. Where the hell is this coming from? All because I'm a little nervous over seeing a pretty woman again. This is ridiculous." I squeezed my eyes shut, trying to get my bearings as Willow droned on, her voice coming at me as though through a thick wall.

"Tyler? Tyler, look at me."

Her hand squeezed my arm. I concentrated on that feeling and tried to refocus. My heart was pounding. What the hell had just happened?

"Are you okay?"

I concentrated on her face, and gradually the roaring in my head eased up and all the little noises in the room became distinct again. The conversations of the other patrons, the soft clinking of silverware touching plates, the music playing from the ceiling, just loud enough to talk over. I looked down at the black tablecloth and was somewhat surprised to find myself still sitting there with my food untouched before me.

"Tyler? Are you with me?"

"Yeah, yeah." I rubbed my temples again. "Sorry, I don't know what happened there."

Her eyes traveled over my face, and then she smiled. "It's okay. It was my fault. I'm sorry. I didn't mean to upset you. Really."

"I know. It's okay."

She picked up her fork. "I really am sorry, Ty. I can tell you're stressed and I'm just adding to it. I wouldn't freak out about it."

Her calm demeanor washed over me. My stomach growled, and I followed her lead, digging into my food. "Yeah, I think you're right." Those days I'd lost not too long ago flashed through my mind, but I pushed it aside. It was probably just low blood sugar mixed with my temper rising or something. I'd be fine once I got some food in me.

Ready for more?
Read Be With Me HERE

ABOUT THE AUTHOR

Hi! My name is Angel Rayne and I write dark, delicious romance with antiheroes who would burn down the world to save the woman they love. I never understood why the villains never win the girl, and so I decided to write them their own love stories where they do.

 Here are a few other odds and ends about me...

-Music inspires my stories and I make playlists for every book.

-I am not a fast writer. My stories take time to write. They need to brew in my head. To have book releases close together I have to write ahead. But I would much rather take the time the stories need to be the best they can be than try to rush them out. Trust me on this one.

-I love the rain, and I'm happiest when I'm sitting in a coffee shop with my laptop as it storms outside.

-I prefer to go watch movies alone, with one of those fancy coffees hidden in my purse. (Yes, I really do this.)

-My husband calls me his "little bird" because anything that sparkles catches my eye.

-I will never have enough soft blankets. Ever.

-I love ALL THE DRAMA...but only in books.

-I will forever re-watch The Phantom of the Opera with the hope that by some miracle, this time Christine will choose the right guy.

Thank you for reading my stories, and I always love to hear from you! You can reach me at: angel@angelrayne.com

www.ingramcontent.com/pod-product-compliance
Lightning Source LLC
Chambersburg PA
CBHW060916190726
48286CB00002B/526